Jon Athan

For more information on this book or the author, please visit www.jon-athan.com. General inquiries are welcome.

Facebook:
https://www.facebook.com/AuthorJonAthan
Twitter: @Jonny_Athan
Email: info@jon-athan.com

Book cover by Sean Lowery:
http://indieauthordesign.com

Thank you for the support!

ISBN-13: 978-1987696165
ISBN-10: 1987696166

First Edition!

WARNING

This book contains scenes of intense violence and some disturbing themes. Some parts of this book may be considered violent, cruel, disturbing, or unusual. This book is *not* intended for those easily offended or appalled. Please enjoy at your own discretion.

Table of Contents

Chapter One

A Reunion

"It's so lonely out here," Gina Tomita said as she stared out the passenger window. "Dark, cold, and lonely. Who would want to take a vacation out here?"

From the driver's seat, his fingers firmly wrapped around the steering wheel, Dominic Torres said, "First of all, it's dark because it's nighttime. Secondly, it's cold because it's nighttime. Lastly, it's lonely because... Well, can you guess why it's lonely out here?"

Gina smiled, rolled her eyes, and said, "Because it's nighttime."

"*Exactly.* These roads, these woods... This whole place is probably going to be filled with annoying douchebags during the day. College kids, pretentious families, lovey-dovey couples... You know, the type of people who ruin vacations for others."

"Hey, what are you trying to say? What's wrong with lovey-dovey couples?"

Dominic huffed, then he said, "Ask me again in a couple of hours. You'll see what I mean after we get to the cabin."

Gina ran her eyes over Dominic's body. Dominic was thirty-three years old. His black hair was cut high-and-tight, wavy on the top and buzz cut on the sides. His face was clean-shaved, revealing his well-defined jawline. His brown eyes gave off a benevolent, welcoming aura. He wore a black jacket over a gray hooded sweatshirt, black jeans, and matching sneakers—*nothing special.*

Feeling her eyes on him, Dominic looked over at Gina with a grin on his face. Gina was the same age as Dominic—thirty-three. Her straight black hair, silky and smooth, reached down to her chin. Her brown eyes were dark but gentle. She was a foot shorter than her boyfriend, standing an even five feet tall. She wore a hooded parka jacket over a thin sweatshirt, jeans, and high-heeled boots.

Dominic asked, "What are you looking at?"

"Nothing."

"Nothing? Come on, you're looking right at me. What? Do I have something on my face?"

"It's nothing. Just keep your eyes on the road."

Gina giggled and shook her head as she pushed on his chin, forcing him to look forward. She actually wanted to say something along the lines of: *I just love you so much.* She didn't want to act like a lovey-dovey couple, though. She turned in her seat and stared out the passenger window again, her eyes narrowed as if she were looking for something.

Their black sedan sped down the desolate road, solely led by their headlights. A few cabins could be seen from the main road, hidden in a sea of trees, bushes, and mud. The cabins looked vacant, though. Vehicles occupied most of the driveways, but the lights were off in the cabins. The night was still young, so it felt unusual and eerie.

Gina asked, "Do you think they're even going to be home?"

"Of course they are. They invited us to this party,

Gina. Why wouldn't they be home?"

"I don't know. It's just... some of these other cabins look empty."

"They probably are empty. It's Friday night. People will start getting here in a few hours or by tomorrow morning."

"Yeah, I guess you're right," Gina said, a pinch of doubt in her voice. She turned in her seat and looked out the windshield. She smiled and said, "I can't believe we're actually going to a 'reunion party' hosted by Brian and Harper. I *never* thought this would happen."

"Me neither. To be honest, I can't say I'm really excited about it."

"I'm not excited to see them, but... I'm thinking of it as an all-expense-paid vacation. We really only have to spend tonight with them at this little party, then we can spend the rest of the weekend doing our own thing. We can go for a hike, we can swim in the lake, we can go for a boat ride. The party might not be so bad, either, especially if they invited a lot of people. It could be like our college days."

Dominic responded, "Yeah, I guess it doesn't sound so bad. You know Brian, though. He's... *different.* He's rich, but he acts like he's not. He acts like he's like the rest of us, except he can afford anything he wants. He doesn't have to worry about bills and all of this 'normal people'-shit."

Gina pouted and nodded. She agreed with Dominic's assessment of Brian's personality. Brian was a wealthy man who acted like a nice older brother around his friends. He always offered a helping hand, even when no one was asking for help.

He exaggerated his friends' issues just to offer his help. Although his intentions were pure, he came off as annoying and pretentious.

Dominic continued, "I really hope he doesn't act like he did us a favor by bringing us out here. I didn't ask for an invitation. Did you?"

"Nope. I found it in my email one morning," Gina responded. She sighed, then she asked, "Who do you think is going to be there? I mean, you talk like you hate him, but we're still going. I'm not sure if everyone from our old circle is as... 'lenient' as us, though. What if... Oh, damn, what if we're the only ones who show up? We'd have to spend the *whole* weekend with them, wouldn't we?"

Dominic chuckled, then he said, "Yup. And I don't think 'lenient' is the right word. We're pushovers, hun, and we can only blame ourselves for our descent into hell." He gently pushed on the brake pedal, allowing the car to roll to a stop. He looked at Gina and said, "No turning back after we make this turn. You sure you want to do this?"

Gina leaned forward and looked past Dominic. The long driveway to the left sloped down to a cozy two-story cabin. The cabin was located far from the main road, but the lights were on, so it was visible from afar. They could sense the sheer affluence in the cabin with a mere glance. It looked expensive, it felt unattainable.

Gina said, "Let's do it."

"Aye aye, captain."

Dominic pushed down on the gas pedal and turned the steering wheel. The car rocked left and right for a few seconds, then it rolled smoothly down the driveway.

***

Jackson Blair leaned over the kitchen island, his rough elbows planted on the countertop. He couldn't help but smirk as he watched Brian Reeves pull a few beer bottles out of the fridge. *Coronas,* he thought, *come on, Brian, we both know you can afford much more.* He was amused, but he decided to bite his tongue.

At thirty-five years old, Jackson stood six-one with a burly physique. He had wide shoulders, a broad chest, and thick arms. His hair was buzz cut, nearly bald, while his beard was long and wild. His blue eyes were lively, bright and zany. He wore a tight gray t-shirt that complemented his muscles, blue jeans, and black boots.

Brian was the polar opposite of Jackson, although the men were the same age. He stood five-eight with a plain physique—not fat but not muscular. His brown hair was wavy and his stubble was patchy. His blue eyes were dim and hollow, like the eyes of a depressed person. Yet, he smiled that fake, happy smile of his. He wore a white button-up shirt, black slacks, and leather and fur loafers—all high-end brands.

Brian closed the door with a kick while awkwardly balancing four bottles of beer in his arms. He placed the bottles on the island, grinning.

He said, "Like I was saying when you got here, man: it's been a while, hasn't it? I mean, do you even remember the last time we saw each other? Like, *really* saw each other?"

Jackson responded, "Yeah. It was five years ago at

a party at your, um, *penthouse.* You know, since you prefer to live in the clouds instead of in a normal apartment like the rest of us. You started throwing your money around after you got your promotion, you acted like a total douche, then we just sort of split ways. Right?"

Brian's left eye and the left side of his mouth twitched with anxiety, but he didn't stop smiling. Jackson answered in a matter-of-factly tone. *'Yeah, it's been a long time,' would have been good enough, Jack,* Brian thought.

He stuttered, "The–The cabin is, um... It's pretty nice, isn't it? There's enough room for all of us, it's near the lake, and there aren't any neighbors in sight. It'll be perfect for our reunion weekend."

Jackson glanced around the kitchen, running his eyes over the expensive appliances and countertops. He looked at the ceiling and thought about the bedrooms. *The rooms are probably bigger and better than our entire apartment,* he thought. He didn't have the opportunity to unpack since Brian personally took his bags upstairs while Harper Reeves—Brian's wife—served them some alcohol.

Jackson said, "It's a real nice place, Brian. I like it more than the penthouse. It's not as, um... douchey. I can't believe you actually bought this place, though. Shit, man, if you're throwing money around, you should give us a loan. Hell, let us move in here while you're not around. It can work like a timeshare, except, you know, we won't pay you."

Jackson chuckled as he leaned away from the island. He wasn't seriously asking for a loan or shelter, he was just joking. Brian misconstrued the message. His nervous grin turned into a slight smile and he didn't laugh.

Brian said, "Hey, man, you know I'm here for you. If you ever need anything, anything at all, just tell me and I'll get it done."

Jackson stopped laughing. He said, "I was kidding, Brian. I know you don't have the best social skills, shit like this goes over your head, but I was joking."

The room became quiet, dominated by tension. Only a woman's muffled voice entered the kitchen through the gaps under the doors.

Jackson furrowed his brow and asked, "You know I was kidding, right? We don't need your charity, okay?"

Brian nodded and said, "Yeah, I know. I was joking, too."

"Oh, so you're *not* offering to help us out?"

"Huh? No, tha–that's not what I meant. I'm–"

"I'm messing with you," Jackson interrupted. He opened two bottles of beer, then he grabbed both with one hand. He said, "Let's go chat with the girls. You're just too awkward and... and out of touch when you're by yourself. Maybe Harper can help you loosen up. Let's go."

Brian couldn't tell if Jackson was genuinely insulting him. He refused to confront him about it, though. So, he bit his bottom lip and nodded in agreement. He popped the caps off the other beers and followed Jackson into the living room.

The living room was wide and spacious, decorated with authentic wood furniture. Expensive electronics—a 4K ultra-high definition television, a surround sound system, and the gist—helped modernize the old cabin. Two leather sofas, a three-seater and a two-seater, and a recliner were located at the center of the room.

Harper Reeves and Vanessa Frazier, thirty-two and thirty years old respectively, sat on the three-seat sofa. The women appeared to be discussing the lake.

Harper was a raven-haired woman with light blue eyes. Her face was round and soft. Although it was barely noticeable, her belly protruded a few inches forward. She was fifteen weeks pregnant, but she tried to hide her pregnancy. Her thin blue house-dress reached down to her thighs and her fluffy slippers protected her feet.

Tied in a ponytail, Vanessa's long black hair swung down around the center of her back. She was short, curvy, and proud. She wore a brown jacket over a little black dress and a pair of high heels.

Jackson handed a bottle to Vanessa, then he took a seat on the two-seat sofa. He raised his beer and tilted it at the women, as if to say: *cheers.* Vanessa snickered as she followed his lead. Brian handed a beer to Harper while taking a swig of his own.

Harper clenched her jaw and gave him an icy glare. *You know damn well I can't drink that,* she thought. Brian's eyes widened as soon as he realized his mistake. He placed the extra bottle on the coffee table between the sofas and recliner.

Brian said, "Feel free to take that one when you're dry, you two. I'm going to get a cup of water for Harper."

As Brian went to the kitchen, Jackson asked, "What's the matter, Harper? Not a fan of beer anymore? Would you prefer some wine and cheese?"

Harper smiled and said, "I would actually prefer some wine, as a matter of fact, but I still like beer, too. I'm just not in the mood for alcohol tonight."

"I hear you. I thought tonight was going to be more of a 'whiskey and wine'-type of night, especially at your cabin. Why are we drinking liquor store beer?"

"I don't know. We have wine and whiskey in the kitchen and cellar."

"Oh, I think you know why. It's Brian's signature move: act poor around the poor people."

Vanessa let out a sigh of annoyance. She said, "We've been here for less than an hour. Don't start with this already, Jackson."

"I'm just speaking the truth. Right, Harper?"

Harper looked at Jackson, then at Vanessa, then back at Jackson. *Yes*—the word was trapped in her throat, eager to burst out. Before she could respond, someone knocked on the front door.

***

Brian rushed into the living room. He placed the cup of water on the coffee table, then he dashed to the front door down the hall beside the kitchen.

He said, "I think that's Dom and Gina."

Jackson said, "*Finally.* Now we can have a real party."

Brian stopped a meter away from the front door. He closed his eyes and took a deep breath, then he opened the door. As expected, Dominic and Gina had finally arrived, bags slung over their shoulders.

Brian enthusiastically said, "Dominic! Gina! I'm glad you could join us."

Dominic responded, "We're glad to be here, Brian. We–"

Mid-sentence, Brian grabbed Dominic's hand and pulled him in for a big hug. He even patted his back and shook his hand while doing so. He did the same to Gina.

Dominic smiled nervously and said, "Like I was saying, we're looking forward to the weekend."

"Yeah, man, it's going to be great," Brian said. He stepped aside and beckoned to the couple. He said, "Come in, come in. Give me your bags, I'll take 'em up to your room, then I'll show you around after dinner."

Dominic and Gina glanced at each other, communicating without saying a word—*no turning back.* They reluctantly handed their bags to Brian and entered the cabin.

While Brian took the bags to a bedroom on the second floor, Dominic and Gina were greeted by Jackson, Vanessa, and Harper. They spoke about their drive to the cabin, the cabin itself, and their lives. They drank, chattered, and laughed, celebrating life with friends and alcohol. Ten minutes had passed, but they didn't notice Brian had already returned to the living room.

As Jackson spoke about the woods—recounting a story of aimless travels—Brian grabbed Dominic's arm and pulled him aside. He tried to lead him into the kitchen, but Dominic stopped him at the doorway. Dominic simply didn't want to be alone with Brian. He wanted to be able to see and hear his friends.

Dominic asked, "What's up, Brian? Something on

your mind?"

Brian said, "Well, I just wanted to talk to you in private. We're more honest when we're not surrounded by so many people. You know what I'm saying?"

"Yeah, I get it. What's on your mind?"

"Um... How are you and Gina doing?"

Dominic narrowed his eyes and cocked his head back. He thought: *that's it? That's what you wanted to ask me?*

He responded, "We're doing fine."

"Good, good. I'm happy to hear that, man. So, how's business? Are your sales still good?"

"Are my sales still good?" Dominic repeated in disbelief. "Brian, we're doing fine. We're okay, really."

"Okay, alright. I just wanted to extend a helping hand. If you need anything—money, shelter, connections—I'm here for you."

Dominic was offended by Brian's offer, but he wasn't surprised. He expected him to flaunt his wealth in a pseudo-altruistic manner. *I don't need a handout,* he thought, *we don't need anything from you.* He didn't want to cause a scene. He wanted to survive the night and spend the rest of the weekend with his girlfriend—nothing more, nothing less.

He sighed, then he said, "Let's just get back to the others. I'm sure Jackson has a lot of stories to tell."

Brian watched as Dominic returned to the group. He was disappointed in himself, but he couldn't help it. Although his actions were seen as insincere, his offers were always genuine. He wanted to help in any way possible, but his delivery sounded condescending. Still, he picked himself up and moved forward. He forced a smile and returned to the party, hoping to salvage the night.

Chapter Two

Like Old Times

Dominic sat on the two-seat sofa, a bottle of beer clasped in his hands above his lap. With a thin smile, he stared up at the in-ceiling speakers above him. A smooth bossa nova song played through the speakers. It sounded like something he would have heard in a hipster cafe. He didn't dislike the genre, but it didn't quite fit the tone of the occasion.

Gina, who sat beside him, nudged Dominic's arm with her elbow. With the same slight smile, she gazed into her boyfriend's eyes. The couple shared the same thought: *what kind of reunion party is this?* They chuckled and shrugged, blatantly amused by the situation, then they each took a swig of their drinks.

Dominic leaned forward in his seat and attempted to rejoin the ongoing conversation. On the three-seat sofa to his left, Vanessa and Harper sat beside each other and discussed the cabin's sauna. Jackson sat at the other end of the sofa and Brian sat on the recliner directly across from Dominic, a long oak coffee table between them.

Brian and Jackson appeared to be discussing online businesses—*entrepreneurship.* Instead of offering money, Brian sought to offer advice.

He said, "All I'm saying is: if you're going to join a pyramid scheme, you're going to want to be near the top of that pyramid. You have to be one of the *first* people to join if you want to see real results. But, you want to know what's better than being in a pyramid? Building it from the ground up, *sitting on top of it.*"

Gina asked, "Aren't pyramid schemes illegal?"

Brian shrugged and responded, "They are, but they're all around us still." He shuffled in his seat and shifted his attention to Gina. He said, "When I say 'pyramid schemes,' I'm not talking 'Bernie Madoff'-style stuff. I'm talking more like... like referring people into affiliate marketing. Yes, you still make money off of other people's work, but it's perfectly legal. Hell, you don't even have to refer anyone. You can market yourself and sell 'magical' weight loss tea to a bunch of suckers on Instagram. These so-called models have been doing it for years. The products are a bunch of bullshit, they don't use that shit for themselves, but they're getting paid by the person at the top of the pyramid... and that person is making even more than them."

"It's still shady, isn't it?"

"Yeah, but... but you're right. There is no excuse for shady business. But I'm just talking business, Gina. That's it. I didn't build a pyramid or anything like that."

Jackson joked, "He's telling the truth. If he did build a pyramid, he would have given us a tour already."

Jackson cackled while the rest of the group snickered. They didn't want to disrespect Brian in his own home. To their surprise, Brian took the joke in stride and laughed along. He acted normal.

Changing the subject, Dominic said, "Enough

about business. This is supposed to be a party—a reunion party. So, who else is coming?"

Harper said, "We invited Gene, Victor, Tiffany, and a few other people. The old crew, you know."

"They couldn't make it, though," Brian said. "It was too sudden, too unexpected, and they didn't have time in their schedules. We didn't feel like pushing the date back, either. We, um... We really wanted this."

Jackson asked, "They couldn't come or they didn't *want* to come?

He grinned and chuckled inwardly, proud of himself. The other guests remained quiet while the music played. They felt the tension rising in the room.

Trying to keep his composure, Brian smiled and said, "It was probably both, Jackson. You know how people are."

Jackson puckered his lips and shook his head. He said, "Actually, I don't. How do you see people, Brian?"

"People are... people."

"What the hell is that even supposed to mean?"

"It means..."

Brian couldn't think of the words to respond. He didn't want to sound defensive, but he couldn't think of anything witty to say either. He was pushed to a corner. He glanced at Harper, but she immediately looked away—she let him drown in a sea of discomfort and embarrassment. He felt tears oozing up to his eyelids. *Don't cry,* he thought, *he's just messing with you, you idiot.*

Gina said, "Leave him alone, Jackson. You've been

bullying him all night. I mean, why'd you even come if you were going to be so rude? Are you drunk already or something?"

Jackson chuckled, then he said, "I'm not drunk. I'm just messing with our old friend. You know, I'm testing the waters to see how far I can go."

"I think you've gone far enough already," Vanessa said. "I think Gina's right, too. You're buzzed, aren't you? We're going to have to cut you off before you really get shit-faced."

"Oh, come on," Jackson responded, rolling his eyes in frustration. He looked at Brian and said, "Tell 'em that we're just fucking around, Brian."

Brian opened his mouth to speak, but he couldn't say a word. He wanted to say: *they're right, you're an asshole, Jackson.* The party had barely begun, though. He didn't want to spoil it so soon.

"*Tell 'em,*" Jackson said sternly.

"We were just messing around, as usual," Brian said. He looked at Gina and said, "I appreciate your concern, but I think throwing a word like 'bullying' around is only going to cause more drama. We're not in high school anymore."

Jackson said, "I told you so."

Gina leaned back in her seat and raised her hands over her head, as if she were caught red-handed by the police. Her gesture said: *fine, I won't get involved.* She grabbed her beer and took a sip. The group became quiet again, allowing the mellow music to waft across the cabin without any interruptions.

Dominic coughed to clear his throat, then he asked, "So, are we the only ones who accepted the invitation? Or should we be expecting a few more guests?"

Harper responded, "We got a couple of 'maybes,' but I doubt anyone else will show up tonight. Gene and his wife, Ariel, *might* drop by. You've met his wife, haven't you? She's very–"

Tap, tap, tap—the faint sound of knocking emerged over the music. Then, the doorbell rang three times.

Jackson said, "Maybe that's them."

Brian shook his head and said, "No. No, I don't think so." As he walked to the front door, he muttered, "Who the hell could it be?"

Chapter Three

A Visitor

Brian and Dominic approached the front door and peeked through the peephole while the rest of the group looked at the porch through the kitchen window. A drizzle arrived during their reunion, dousing the area with rain. Yet, through the raindrops rolling down the foggy windows, they could see their uninvited guest standing at the bottom of the porch.

The young man looked to be in his early twenties. His beach blonde hair was wet and wavy, tousled like a movie star's hairdo. His shiny blue eyes could be seen from afar, practically glowing in the dark. His face was chiseled, slim and defined, and his body was lean but hard. He wore a black leather jacket over a white t-shirt, black jeans, and matching boots.

He knocked on the door again, then he stepped off the porch and stared at the windows. He searched for a sign of life in the cabin.

In a low tone, just above a whisper, Brian asked, "Should we answer the door?"

Dominic shrugged and asked, "Why wouldn't we?"

"I don't know. It's strange, isn't it? It's past seven, there's no car outside, no one invited him here, so... what's he doing here?"

"Why don't you open the door and find out?"

From the neighboring doorway, which led to the

kitchen, Jackson said, "You're not scared of that pretty boy, are you, Brian?"

Brian responded, "I'm not scared, I'm just being cautious. It seems dangerous to let a stranger into our cabin."

"I agree," Harper said. "He could be a criminal, he could be crazy."

Chiming in from the kitchen, Gina said, "He could be lost, he could be hurt. Listen, there's six of us, guys. I don't think he can easily rob us."

"And what if he has a gun?" Harper rebutted.

"I, um... I don't know. It doesn't seem like–"

"It doesn't matter what it *seems* like. We don't know anything about him. Opening the door might be the right thing to do, but good Samaritans aren't exactly rewarded for their good deeds nowadays. We've all seen the news. We know what can happen if he's not a good guy."

Her arms crossed, Vanessa asked, "Jackson, do you really think it's a good idea to let him in? *Really?*"

Before Jackson could respond, the visitor knocked again—faster, *harder.* The door rattled in the frame. The young man was clearly strong and eager to get inside.

From the porch, the visitor shouted, "Hello! I need help! I need a phone! Please open the door! It's freezing out here!"

Dominic looked at Brian and said, "It's your cabin, it's your choice. What do you want to do?"

Brian dug his fingers into his hair and sighed. He looked at his friends, hoping someone else would take the lead. To his dismay, his peers waited for his decision.

He said, "Just keep your eyes on him." He turned the locks, then he opened the door. Smiling, he said, "Sorry for the wait. We were, um... We didn't hear you. How can we help you?"

The young man stood in silence, rainwater dripping from the ends of his hair. He looked surprised as he ran his eyes over the group. He could see Brian, Dominic, Jackson, and Harper in the hallway. He leaned to his right and peered through the kitchen doorway. He spotted Vanessa and Gina in the kitchen.

He smiled and said, "I'm sorry, I didn't expect there to be so many of you in here. There's, um... There's only one car in the driveway."

Brian said, "Yeah, that's mine. The others are in the garage. Is that a problem?"

"No, no. I'm just surprised. I didn't expect to interrupt a party. That's all."

"Okay, well... How can we help you?"

"My name is Chase—*Chase Bowen.* My car broke down around a mile down the road. My phone is dead, so I can't call for help. I was wondering if I could use a phone for a few minutes. That's all, okay? I'll be out of your hair in no time."

"You're soaked," Harper said, stretching her neck up from behind the men. "I'll get you a towel."

In the kitchen, Vanessa leaned closer to Gina and whispered, "He's a looker, isn't he? He's like a model straight off a magazine. How old do you think he is?"

"Old enough," Gina joked. The women giggled while nudging each other. Gina said, "Seriously, though. He seems harmless, right?"

"I guess so. He could be a charming psychopath, though. I guess we'll find out. I'll take one for the team and get to know him."

Jackson glanced over his shoulder, his arms crossed as he leaned against the door frame. He huffed and rolled his eyes, annoyed by their conversation.

Brian said, "Okay, come in. I'll, um... I'll go look for my phone. I left it somewhere around here."

"Thank you very much, sir. I really appreciate this," Chase said as he entered the house. "And, again, I'm sorry for interrupting your little get-together."

Vanessa pushed her way past Jackson. With a smirk, she handed her phone to Chase and said, "Forget about it. Here, you can use my phone. I'm Vanessa, by the way."

Under his breath, Jackson muttered, "You're taken, by the way."

Chase accepted the phone and said, "Thank you. I'll get this back to you in a minute."

Harper returned to the front door with a blue towel. She squeezed past her friends and gave it to Chase. While doing so, she caught a glimpse of his blue eyes. She couldn't help but smile and blush. She feared him only a few minutes ago, but she was suddenly attracted to him, like a teenager attracted to a pop star.

Chase returned the smile—an effortless million-dollar smile. He dried his hair with the towel and followed the group to the living room.

He asked, "Can I use your bathroom? I'd like a little bit of privacy while I make this call and, you know, I really have to pee."

Brian shrugged and said, "I guess that wouldn't be a problem. Follow me."

The living room was seamlessly connected to the dining room. The dining area—comprised of a rectangular walnut dining table, a cupboard, and console tables—was located on the right side of the living room. A door in the dining room led to a small bathroom, which only had a toilet, a sink, and a medicine cabinet.

Brian led Chase to that bathroom. Chase locked himself in the room and made his phone call while the group waited for him in the living room. His muffled voice barely seeped past the heavy door.

Brian said, "It's kinda suspicious, isn't it? Why does he need privacy to call a mechanic?"

Dominic responded, "Maybe he's not calling a mechanic. Maybe he can't afford roadside assistance so he's calling his dad or something. It's not *that* suspicious."

Vanessa said, "I don't like it, either. When I offered my phone, I thought he was just going to make a quick call in front of us." She laughed, then she said, "What if he's in there looking at my 'private' pictures right now?"

"I'm sure it's nothing the internet hasn't seen before," Jackson joked. Vanessa huffed and slapped his arm. Jackson said, "Seriously, I heard your carpet is legendary in Japan. Isn't that right, Gina?"

Gina closed her eyes in frustration and said, "We've been through this a million times: I'm Japanese, but I'm not from Japan."

"Okay, okay. My mistake. I thought you would

have seen a little clip of Vanessa's bush online. That's all."

Gina looked back at Jackson, she smirked, and she said, "Well, I have seen it."

Vanessa giggled, then she said, "Fuck off, guys."

Brian ignored their chatter. He kept his eyes glued to the bathroom door. He listened to Chase's muffled voice, trying to identify every word.

Without taking his eyes off the door, he asked, "Did any of you feel strange around him?"

"Strange?" Harper repeated in an uncertain tone. "What do you mean?"

Jackson asked, "Did you get butterflies in your stomach, Brian? Was it love at first sight?"

Brian responded, "No, I mean... He's like the bad guy in a horror movie. He's like the good-looking guy who turns out to be a psycho. Like... Like Mark Wahlberg in *Fear*."

Vanessa said, "We were just talking about that in the kitchen. That's a great movie, right?"

"Yeah, I guess, but... That's who he reminds me of. He's too–"

The bathroom door swung open. Chase stepped into the doorway, the towel around his neck. He looked at the guests, one-by-one, and they looked back at him.

Jackson said, "There's the psycho now, Brian. Why don't you ask him for yourself?"

The side of Brian's mouth twitched as he locked eyes with Chase. He was put on the spot, pushed on stage without a script. He thought: *what do I say? What the hell do I say?*

Chase asked, "Is there a problem?"

Brian stuttered, "N–No, it–it was nothing."

Chase said, "Okay." He leaned over the dining table and extended his hand forward. He said, "Here's your phone, ma'am. Thanks again. I really appreciate it."

Vanessa took the phone from him and said, "No problem. You didn't happen to, you know, look through my pictures, did you?"

"Oh, shut up already, Vanessa," Jackson said, clearly irritated by her flirtatious behavior.

The rest of the group laughed, tickled by their interaction. Vanessa was teasing Chase and Jackson, but she wouldn't mind having a threesome with them. Their relationship, although often plagued by jealousy, was open *and* secure. They were the type of couple to experiment, and the rest of the group was well aware of that.

Chase said, "Anyway, my ride will be here in about an hour. I can make it back to my car in ten, maybe fifteen minutes. It's still raining out there, but I can manage." He handed the towel to Harper and said, "I'm not feeling so cold anymore thanks to you. I appreciate it, ma'am."

Harper bit her bottom lip and nodded. She tried to stop herself from blushing, but she couldn't help herself. Her round cheeks turned pink and her eyes brightened with interest. Brian didn't notice her reaction, though. He was too busy thinking about an appropriate response. He thought: *do I kick him out, should I drive him back to his car, or should I invite him to stay?*

Harper was happy to make the choice for him. She said, "It's raining and it's cold out there. You just warmed up and dried yourself. You should stay for dinner. Then, Brian will give you a ride back to your car. Okay?" She glanced over at the rest of the group and asked, "We're okay with that, right?"

Dominic looked at Gina, Vanessa looked at Jackson, and Brian stared at Harper. Except for Harper, all of them were reluctant. Dominic, Gina, Jackson, and Vanessa didn't have much of a choice, though. They were invited to the party, but it wasn't their cabin. Only Brian had the power to reject the suggestion.

Harper asked, "Is that okay, Brian?"

Brian gritted his teeth, then he said, "Sure, sure. There's plenty of food, drinks, and space."

"That's exactly what I was thinking."

Chase said, "I don't know. It's a very generous offer and I really appreciate it, but... you barely know me and I barely know you. It feels... exploitative. I don't want to intrude on your little get-together or ruin your night."

Harper responded, "Exploitative? Not at all. We insist, Chase. Please join us. I think it'll be fun."

Chase looked at the group. He saw a small crowd of friendly, welcoming faces. His eyes stopped on Brian. Brian stared at Chase with an expression of concern—straight lips, worried eyes, a steady face. His eyes said: *I don't trust you, I don't want you here, please leave my house.* Brian wasn't the confrontational type, though.

Chase shrugged and said, "Well, I guess I've got an hour to spare. What's for dinner?"

Brian lowered his head and exhaled in disappointment while the rest of the group welcomed Chase to the cabin with open arms. *I can handle it,* he thought, *everything's okay, we're fine.*

Chapter Four

Dinner

Dinner was prepared before the guests had arrived, but the food was still fresh and warm. The meal consisted of juicy steak, creamy mashed cauliflower, garlicky roasted broccoli, and baked sweet potato fries. There was a glass of red wine beside each plate —except for Harper's cup, which was filled with water. The heavenly scent of the food rose to the ceiling, lingering above the guests during the entire meal.

The dining table sat eight people—three on each long side, one at each short end. Chase sat at one end of the table and Harper sat at the other. In order from closest to farthest, Vanessa, Jackson, and Brian sat to Chase's left. To his right, Dominic sat in the middle seat and Gina sat in the seat closest to Harper. The seat directly to Chase's right was vacant. The party-goers had already introduced themselves before they started eating.

Harper took a sip of her water, then she said, "So, now that we're all acquainted, what exactly were you doing out here, Chase? Are you on a trip? Or are you staying nearby?"

Harper's last question sounded hopeful, as if she hoped he would answer with a resounding 'yes.' She thought about the things she could do with him if he were staying in a neighboring cabin.

Chase held a closed fist over his mouth as he

swallowed his food, then he said, "I'm staying nearby. My friends and I rented a cabin down the road. Well, *somewhere* down the road. To be honest with you, I never found it. I drove around in circles for an hour or two, then my car just died on me." He stabbed his steak and said, "I was hoping, by some miracle, my friends would have answered that door when I knocked. They could have taken me back to my car, I would have grabbed my stuff, then I would have gone back to the cabin and relaxed. You know, I could have started my vacation. I'm glad I found you, though. You've been very kind to me. Much kinder than my friends, actually."

Dominic said, "Your closest friends are sometimes your worst enemies. Just look at Jackson and Brian. They would have killed each other if we weren't around."

"No way," Jackson said. He took a bite of his steak. With a full mouth, he said, "Brian couldn't kill me if my hands and legs were tied. Shit, he'd probably end up killing himself before he even scratched me."

The group shared a laugh at Brian's expense. Brian smiled and shrugged as he stared down at his plate. The joke didn't hurt him. He only thought about Harper and their new guest.

As the room settled, Chase asked, "What's your situation? Hmm? A couples retreat? A housewarming party? An orgy?"

Jackson leaned back in his seat and cackled. Vanessa looked at her boyfriend with wide eyes, surprised by his laughter. Dominic and Gina glanced at each other, communicating with their eyes—*sounds like an interesting idea, doesn't it?* Harper lowered her head and snickered. Brian remained quiet and distant, present at the table but separated from the conversation.

Jackson said, "I'm not saying I love any of you, but an orgy would be nice. It would definitely help break the tension around here. I heard orgies create everlasting bonds, too. It's true."

"Shut up, Jackson," Vanessa said before taking a bite of a fry.

Gina explained, "Sorry to disappoint you, Chase, but we're not having an orgy. Not tonight, at least. This was supposed to be a reunion party, then we were going to spend the weekend together."

Chase said, "I see, a reunion party... You must have been separated for a while to be having a reunion. What's the story behind that?"

"Well, except for Vanessa, we all met in college around fourteen or fifteen years ago. After graduating, we lived in the same city, we mingled in the same circles... but we just really haven't been together for the last four years."

"Why?"

A dead silence followed the intrusive question. The joyful atmosphere was replaced with a gloomy ambiance. The appetizing scent of the food even miraculously vanished.

Chase said, "I'm sorry. That's too personal, isn't it?"

Dominic responded, "There is no 'why.' Some people just naturally grow apart because of work and life. That's just how it works." He pointed at Brian and said, "Thankfully, Brian got ahold of us after buying this cabin and he brought us together again. He gave us an opportunity to build bridges again. I think that's great. I really do."

"I agree," Chase said. He took a swig of his wine, then he said, "I'm sorry to change the subject so drastically and this might be personal, too, but... I heard you say Brian *bought* this cabin. What kind of work do you have to do to buy such an expensive place?"

Brian did not respond. He stabbed his steak with a fork, lost in the labyrinthine crevices of his mind.

Harper leaned closer to him and said, "Honey, he asked you a question."

Still staring down at his plate, Brian asked, "What kind of work do *you* do to be able to rent a cabin nearby, Chase?"

Chase responded, "I think the cabin we rented cost about one-hundred and forty-five dollars a night. It's not nearly as expensive as *buying* a vacation home, but it's still a pretty penny, especially when you're staying for seven days. Fortunately for me, I didn't have to pay a dime. My buddy paid for everything. The rent, the boats, the food, the booze... Everything."

"So, what does *he* do?"

"He's a pusher. A drug dealer, you know?"

Stony-faced, Brian turned away from his plate and glared at Chase. The rest of the group followed his lead, staring at their guest with curious eyes. Chase looked back at them with a deadpan expression—a steady, unwavering face—then he chuckled and clapped. He took a bite of his steak and sipped his wine.

He said, "I was joking, guys. Just trying to lighten

the mood. I apologize if I somehow frightened or offended you. Really, I'm sorry."

Harper smiled and said, "Oh, you didn't scare us. You just... surprised us. You're a charming guy, we didn't expect you to be funny, too."

Brian gritted his teeth as he retreated from the conversation. He continued angrily stabbing his steak. He thought: *charming? Funny? He's none of that, Harper.*

Jackson said, "Brian bought this cabin a year ago. Paid for it in full with cold, hard cash. You believe that?"

Chase said, "It's hard to believe since a lot of these cabins are rentals, but it is impressive. I'm actually starting to think Brian might be a drug dealer himself... or maybe a politician. You know, the type to say he cares about the little guy and vilify the rich while being selfish and filthy rich himself. I can't help but wonder how lavish your actual home might be, Brian. Hell, I'm starting to wonder how many houses you actually own. Two? Three? Five? Or do you–"

"What are you trying to say? What's your point?" Brian interrupted.

Smirking, Chase shrugged and responded, "I don't know. Maybe I'm just curious, maybe I'm just looking for financial advice. I might be looking for a... a mentor." He chuckled and shook his head. He said, "I just want to know: what do you do?"

"I... I work. I work a lot. And I make the... the correct decisions in life. That's all there is to it."

Jackson cocked his head back upon hearing the response. He turned in his seat and scowled at

Brian, clearly offended.

He asked, "What are *you* trying to say, Brian? Huh? You saying people, like blue-collar people, don't make the 'correct' decisions? You're saying we don't work a lot?"

"You know that's not what I meant."

"What else could it mean? You just said you're rich because you make the right choices, didn't you? You implied that the rest of us don't."

"I said something like that, but that's not what I insinuated. I just answered the damn question."

Dominic waved and said, "Calm down, guys. Now's not the time."

"Relax, Jack," Vanessa said as she tugged on her boyfriend's arm. She grabbed his glass of wine and slid it away from his plate. She said, "It's the alcohol, sweetie. It's messing with your head. He didn't mean anything by it, really."

Jackson still glared at Brian—hot-faced and red-eyed. His clenched fist was planted on the table, ready to knock Brian off his seat at a moment's notice. Brian gazed into Jackson's eyes, then he looked down at his fist, and then back at his eyes. *Just hit me already,* he thought, *knock me out so we can move on with the night.*

Chase leaned forward in his seat and said, "Dominic's right. He's completely right. We should calm down. I didn't mean to cause any trouble for any of you. I'm just a naturally curious person and sometimes I can't control my tongue. I'm sure all of you are good people. I wouldn't be here if you weren't. I'm sorry and... and thanks again for welcoming me to your cabin."

Chase raised his glass—*cheers.* Dominic, Gina, and Vanessa followed his lead. Jackson's wine was taken away, so he just nodded in agreement. Brian scratched the back of his head and sighed in disappointment. Harper gazed at Chase with lascivious eyes. She thought: *what else can your tongue do?*

Chase lowered his glass and said, "The food was great, compliments to the chef, but it looks like my time is running out. So, how about we play a party game? Hmm? I know a lot of 'em and I think it'll really lighten the mood. It might even be therapeutic."

Harper asked, "What are you thinking? Hide and seek?"

"No, no. I'm thinking... 'two truths and a lie.' It's easy, it's quick, and it's fun. Sound good?"

The group sang a song of puffing and sighing, but none of them rejected the idea. After the heated dinner, they needed a break.

Chapter Five

Two Truths and a Lie

Chase asked, "Have all of you played 'two truths and a lie' before?" The group answered with a 'yes'—except for Brian. Chase asked, "Brian, have you played before?"

Staring down at the dining table, Brian responded, "No."

"No? Damn, you must have had a... boring childhood. It's okay, though. It's fine. It gives me the opportunity to explain the rules. So, each player has to come up with two truths and one lie about themselves and the objective of the game is to find out which one is the lie. The person who identifies the lie gets to go next. If two or more people identify it, then I'll pick the next player. Now, if *no one* discovers the lie, you all lose the game and I get to pick another one."

"Another what?" Jackson asked, his brow raised in confusion.

"Another party game."

"Why would you want to pick another game? You don't plan on spending the night with us, do you?"

Chase chuckled, then he said, "I don't plan on it, no. But, if it happens, it happens. A few party games never hurt anyone, right?"

The guests muttered amongst themselves. There was an air of uncertainty in the room, but, yet again, none of them rejected the suggestion.

Vanessa said, "I guess it could be fun. I mean, it's not like we had other plans anyway. We probably would have ended up playing some old party games eventually."

Gina said, "If not, we all would have ended up on our phones, looking through Facebook and Instagram. This sounds good. Let's just try not to get carried away."

Chase said, "So, we all agree. I have one more rule, though: you cannot respond when your significant others are telling their truths and lies. For example: Vanessa, you can't respond when Jackson is telling his truths and lies. You can't give any hints, either. You know too much and it would be too easy. We want this to be fair, don't we?"

Except for Brian, who sulked at the table, the group agreed to Chase's rules. It seemed like a fair and balanced game—simple, clean, and harmless.

Chase said, "Let's begin with you, Jackson."

Jackson shrugged, then he said, "Okay. Let's see, um... I drove here but my license is suspended, I've lost fifteen pounds of fat in the last four months, and I once puked while listening to a shitty pop song on the radio."

"Oh, God," Gina said as she rolled her eyes.

Dominic smiled and said, "I really hope you didn't drive with a suspended license."

A big grin on his face, Jackson asked, "Well, what do you think?"

Gina said, "The first one is the lie. You're a daring guy, you can be an idiot sometimes, but you wouldn't take that risk."

"I agree," Dominic said.

Harper said, "I'm going to go with the pop song. There's no way that happened."

Chase said, "Don't be a party-pooper, Brian. What's your guess?"

Brian sucked his lips into his mouth and breathed deeply through his nose. He glanced around the table—all eyes were on him.

He said, "The first one. It has to be the first one."

Jackson looked at all of his peers, his head rocking back and forth like a bobble-head toy. He savored the attention, purposely waiting to announce the results.

He said, "I'm a big man, but I'm getting leaner. All that hard work at the gym has been paying off." He lifted his right arm and flexed his bulging bicep. He chuckled, then he said, "I puked while listening to some crappy song on the radio, too. I was drunk that night, but I think the song had something to do with it. I really do."

"Crap," Harper said. "I guess I'm out."

Chase said, "So that means we have three winners. I think... Dominic should go next." He nodded at Dominic and said, "You said you were a writer when we met, didn't you? You sound like a *very* interesting person. Go on. Tell the truth."

Dominic said, "Sure, sure. How about this... One of my books is currently being optioned to be made into a movie, I drank an entire pot of coffee one morning that sent me to the doctor because of a very bad anxiety attack, and... and I'm not getting tired of writing."

Gina furrowed her brow upon hearing her boyfriend's last statement. She knew his first two statements were true, which meant his last statement was a lie. *He's tired of writing,* she thought, *why didn't he ever mention it before?* Throughout their entire relationship, she had never heard him complain about his career—*never.*

She looked around the table. Her friends submitted their choices, but she didn't hear a word. The revelation was jarring.

Chase asked, "So, what's the lie, Dominic?"

Dominic drummed his fingertips on the table and said, "One of my novels *is* being optioned. It might become a movie, it might not. Either way, it feels good to be in this position. It feels like I've accomplished something."

"Congrats," Jackson said. "You deserve it, bud."

Vanessa said, "You know I haven't read any of your books, but I won't miss the movie. Congratulations, Dom."

Dominic laughed inwardly, then he said, "Thank you, thank you." *Hmm*—the sound seeped past his lips as he thought about his next explanation. He said, "Anyway, I did go to the doctor after drinking that pot of coffee. It was embarrassing, but at least I know I don't have arrhythmia."

Chase said, "So, that means you *are* becoming bored of writing. A young writer who's tired of writing... I knew you were interesting." He smirked at Harper and said, "I guess that means you were right, ma'am."

Harper smiled and said, "I just picked the one no one else did. A lucky guess."

"Yeah, lucky... So, it's your turn."

Before Harper could say another word, Gina

turned towards Dominic and asked, "Why didn't you ever tell me you were tired of writing? Tired of your... your career?"

Dominic responded, "I don't know. I didn't want you to worry and I didn't think it was a big deal."

"This is your career we're talking about, Dominic. Of course it's a big deal."

"My book is being optioned and I have a backlist. I think we'd be fine if I took a sabbatical."

"Okay, well... It's something we should talk about, isn't it? We're in this together. We're–"

"Sorry to interrupt, but we're in the middle of a game here," Chase said. "We're trying to avoid drama anyway, remember?"

Gina said, "Whatever. Let's keep playing then."

Chase said, "Okay. Your turn, Harper."

Harper slid her tongue across her pearly-white teeth while staring down at the table. Her eyes were contemplative, narrowed with curiosity. She had a lot to say, but she didn't know how to say it.

She drew a deep, shuddery breath, then she said, "Okay, here it goes. I am very happy to have all of you here today, including you, Chase. I am very happy with Brian. And, finally... I'm pregnant. That's it. Those are my two truths and my one lie."

Jackson formed the perfect 'o' with his mouth, then he laughed. Vanessa's jaw dangled open as she glanced around the table, looking for direction during the awkward moment. Dominic and Gina gazed into each other's eyes, surprised. Their eyes said: *oh, shit.*

Brian shook his head and whimpered, tears welling in his eyes. He knew the answer, he knew the truth. He just didn't know how to react to it.

Chase grinned and asked, "So, what are your answers?"

Dominic didn't want to be the last person to answer. He figured it would be too tense and awkward if he waited.

He cracked a nervous smile and said, "You look great, Harper. There's no way you're pregnant."

Gina nodded rapidly and stuttered, "I–I agree."

Avoiding eye contact, Vanessa said, "The last one. The last one is the lie."

Jackson squinted at Harper and Brian, analyzing them with a pair of observant eyes. He tried to read their body language, but to no avail. Although not quite inebriated, he was buzzed due to the alcohol flowing through his system. He didn't notice the fear and sadness in Brian's eyes, he didn't recognize the confusion and frustration in Harper's voice.

Jackson said, "I'm guessing you two aren't actually happy to see us. I felt it as soon as we walked into this cabin. It all felt so... so fake. That's your lie, isn't it?"

Harper didn't respond. Her fingers, thin and manicured, trembled gently on the table. *Say something,* she thought, *move on with your life.*

As he looked around the table, Chase said, "Interesting choices. None of you picked her second statement—she's happy with Brian—so you might lose this round. Then again, they're the perfect couple, aren't they? I guess we'll find out the truth, won't we?" He looked at Harper, the corner of his mouth rising in a sly grin. He asked, "So, who was right, Harper?"

Harper held her hand over her mouth and cried. She snorted and wheezed as tears rolled down her cheeks. She smiled, then she frowned, then she smiled again. She couldn't control her emotions. One part of her felt happy and liberated while the other part of her felt cold and dead. It was like she lost a child while simultaneously giving birth to a new baby.

Her voice cracking, she said, "I am fifteen weeks pregnant. I guess it's not too noticeable, but it's true. I'm also... I'm..." She paused to swallow the lump in her throat. She said, "I'm also happy to see all of you. You don't know how much this means to me. I missed you so much."

Harper took a sip of her water, hoping to drown her emotional pain, but the effort was fruitless. She slammed the cup on the table and sobbed. Tears glistened on her cheeks, mucus filled her nostrils, and saliva flooded her mouth. She mumbled about her relationship and her mistakes, but her words were slurred.

Gina and Vanessa rushed to her side. They tried to comfort her, rubbing her shoulders while whispering words of reassurance into her ears—*it's okay, everything's going to be fine.*

Chase turned his attention to Brian. He watched as Brian sniffled and cried by his lonesome. None of his friends ran to his side. He was abandoned, shunned by the group.

Chase asked, "Brian, what's the real reason for this party? Huh? Did you want to show off your wealth? Did you want to announce your pregnancy to people you haven't spoken to in years? Were you trying to fix your broken relationship? Or... Or was it a little of everything?"

"I never wanted any of this," Brian responded. "I just wanted a reunion. I wanted to... to be around friendly people. That's all, I swear."

Chase asked, "Does anyone else have children?" He glanced around the table. He asked, "Anyone? *Anyone?*"

As she rubbed Harper's shoulder, Vanessa said, "I was pregnant a few years ago. I had a miscarriage. Before you ask: yes, Brian and Harper knew about it. I also know they wouldn't do something like this to 'show off.' I'm not jealous or bitter or anything like that. I'm happy for Harper, okay?"

Chase furrowed his brow and asked, "You're happy that Harper is pregnant with the child of a man she does *not* love?"

"That's not what I meant."

"That's what it sounded like."

"Why are you twisting my words?"

"I'm not twisting your words. I'm making you stand by them. 'I'm happy for Harper,' that's what you said right after she confessed to being miserable. I didn't make those words come out of your mouth, did I? You can argue about my interpretation, but... honestly, you don't have a leg to stand on."

Brian glared at Chase and said, "I think it's time you left. Get out of my house."

Chase huffed and shook his head, amused by the demand. He wasn't afraid of Brian. He knew the short, scrawny man couldn't hurt him. He was worried about Jackson's reaction to his defiance, the man was a brute, but he figured he could handle him thanks to the alcohol. He didn't see a single threat at the dining table.

He said, "We had a deal. No one won the last round, Brian, so that means I get to pick another party game. All of you agreed to the rules and I can't let you break them."

Tears dripping from his eyes with each blink, Brian sternly repeated, "Get out of my house."

"If you win the next game, I–"

"Get out of my damn house!" Brian barked as he slammed his fist on the table.

With his furious roar—his battle cry—the cabin became quiet. Harper even stopped crying upon hearing her husband's booming voice. The guests looked at Brian as if he had transformed into a completely different person before their very eyes. Chase was not impressed by his performance, though.

Tap, tap, tap—someone knocked on the front door three times, then the doorbell rang.

Chase smiled and said, "Oh, they're finally here."

Chapter Six

The Crew

Chase casually walked to the front door, a spring in each step. He behaved as if he owned the place, calm and proud. Brian followed him to the door, eager to get rid of him. Jackson and Dominic approached the hallway while the women stayed near the dining table. They were all baffled by Chase's enigmatic behavior.

As he approached Chase, Brian said, "I want you to get out of my house. *Now.*"

Chase ignored him—*yadda, yadda, yadda.* He turned the locks and opened the door, a cocky grin on his face. Rory Dyer and Hazel Olsen, two twentysomethings, stood on the porch.

A mop of curly hair grew out of Rory's head, corkscrews protruding every which way. His dark brown eyes twinkled with mischief. He had a long nose and a chiseled, clean-shaved face. His body was strong and lean, like Chase's. He wore a gray crewneck sweatshirt under a black jacket, blue jeans, and boots.

At four-eleven, Hazel stood a foot shorter than Rory. She was gutsy, puckish, and strong, though. Her short black hair barely reached down to her chin, decorated with a single purple streak. Her vibrant green eyes could hypnotize any man. She wore a large black jacket, which belonged to Chase, a white tank top, a short black skirt, and knee-high

high-heeled boots.

Although the rain had stopped, the visitors were wet. Hazel's tank top became see-through, revealing her hard nipples, while Rory's hair drooped over his eyes.

With his arms extended away from his body as if he were welcoming a hug, Chase said, "Rory, Hazel, welcome to the party. It took you long enough to get here."

As he entered the cabin, a heavy duffel bag slung over his shoulder, Rory said, "It was a long walk and we had to carry the stuff." He glanced at Hazel, who carried a light backpack. He said, "Okay, *I* had to carry the stuff."

"You're a big boy, Rory. Stop complaining," Hazel said as she followed his lead. "You're lucky I even carried this bag. Chase told you to carry this shit, not me."

Chase closed and locked the door behind them. He said, "She's right, man. I put you in charge of the bags, so stop complaining. Besides, you need the exercise. We can't have you going soft on us."

He grabbed Hazel's waist and pulled her closer to him. He gently bit her bottom lip, then the couple shared a passionate kiss—tongue and all.

Chase said, "At least you're not bitching, baby."

"I can start if you want."

"Actually, that might not be a bad idea. We can argue, then we can fuck. 'Make-up sex,' right?"

"Who are these people?" Brian asked, flustered. "What are they doing in my house? What's going on here?"

Ignoring his host, Chase beckoned to his friends

and said, "We'll talk later, guys. Come on, there's a party in the dining room right now. It was just getting good."

Brian said, "Excuse me. *Excuse me,* but who do you think you are? What do you think you're doing? I'm talking to you, damn it!"

The visitors ignored Brian. Dominic and Jackson returned to the dining table, prepared to defend themselves amidst the intrusion. Rory nodded at the guests and sat on the armrest of the two-seat sofa. Chase entered the living room with his arm over Hazel's shoulders while Hazel kept her hand on his waist. They stopped at the opposite end of the dining table, away from the other guests.

Chase said, "Hey, guys. This is my girlfriend, Hazel, and that's my best friend, Rory. Just for the sake of saving time, allow me to introduce you. I mean, we wouldn't want to bore anyone, would we?" As if he were calling roll in class, he pointed at each guest and said their names: "Dominic, Gina, Harper, Vanessa, Jackson, Brian."

Rory said, "It's nice to meet all of you." As he looked around, his eyes gliding over the expensive furniture, walls, and ceiling, he said, "Nice place you've got here. It's fancy. Cozy. *Safe.*"

Hazel stared at Harper and asked, "Why are you crying, babe? Why do some of you look like you stepped in shit already?" She pouted as she looked up at Chase, pretending to be angry and disappointed. She said, "You were having fun without us, weren't you?"

Chase responded, "We were playing a game of 'two truths and a lie.' Some feelings were hurt, some tears were shed, but they're fine. We had fun, but the night is just getting started."

"Okay, sounds good to me. I never liked 'two truths and a lie' anyway. I prefer 'truth or dare.' It's more exciting."

Teary-eyed, Harper asked, "What's going on, Chase? Where's the mechanic or your ride... or whoever you called?"

Brian approached the table and said, "We want answers."

Chase laughed—a soft, unconcerned laugh—and he looked around the room. He looked at each guest, delighted by the fear in their eyes.

He said, "Okay, okay. I'll tell you the truth... My car *did* break down, but I didn't call a mechanic. You see, as soon as you opened that front door for me, I knew you were all special people—gentle, nice, welcoming. This place was so big and beautiful and we really couldn't find our cabin, so I told my friends to come here for the night. I figured we could have fun together. We're good, right? No hard feelings?"

Jackson huffed, then he muttered, "Unbelievable. Un-*fucking*-believable. Brian always lets people walk all over him, doesn't he?"

Doubt laced in her voice, Gina said, "So, you invited yourself and your friends to our cabin without our permission because... because you wanted to have fun?"

"No. 'Our' is incorrect, Gina. You don't own anything here, except for the clothes on your back and a few bags filled with your belongings," Chase responded. He looked at Brian, who stood to his right. He said, "This is Brian's cabin, paid in full with his cold, hard cash, which he legitimately earned and the rest of you didn't. So, this is okay with you, isn't it, Brian?"

Brian was awed by Chase's casual audacity. For a second, he couldn't actually speak. He could croak, he could groan, but the words wouldn't come out of his mouth. His mind was addled—*overloaded.* He closed his eyes and breathed deeply through his nose. Although he wouldn't throw a punch, he clenched his fists in order to create a semblance of determination.

I will hit you, he thought, *please believe me, please don't push me.* He opened his eyes and glared at the intruders.

Brian said, "It's not okay. I think it might even be illegal."

"Whoa, whoa, whoa," Rory said. "Illegal? That's a strong word, mister."

"Yeah, I know. I think it's accurate, too. This is a–a... a home invasion."

"A home invasion? Are you kidding me? Do we look like we're wearing some shitty animal masks? Did you see us standing in the background and doing nothing to you?"

Chase said, "Rory is right, Brian. That is a serious allegation. Look, man, we're not trying to cause any trouble. We're going to leave very soon. You have my word on that. But, we have some unfinished business to handle first."

Sniffling, Harper asked, "What business? What are you talking about?"

"You lost the game, remember? So you owe me another one."

Brian asked, "What is it with you and your obsession with 'games?' What is all of this?"

Jackson asked, "What is it with you and your obsession with showing off, Brian?"

"Shut up," Brian said without taking his eyes off of Chase.

"What? What did you just say to me, you little punk? I'll rip your head from your–"

"*Quiet,*" Harper said, her eyes closed in frustration. "Just be quiet."

She opened her eyes and glanced around. She thought about her friends and the intruders. At the moment, the situation was manageable. Chase and his friends were pushing their luck, but they didn't harm or threaten anyone. *He's a nice young man,* she thought, *he doesn't want to hurt us, he just wants to play.*

Harper said, "Chase, we welcomed you to our home, but that doesn't give you the right to invite people here without our permission. Illegal or not, it's wrong and disrespectful." As Chase opened his mouth to speak, she held her index finger up, as if to say: *be quiet, I am speaking.* She continued, "But, we had a deal. We'll play your game if you agree to leave afterward. Okay?"

Chase puckered his lips, then he said, "Fine. We'll leave soon."

"I'm serious. If you don't leave, if you do anything we don't want you to do, we will call the cops."

"Okay, okay. I get it. You're the leader, ma'am. Your house, your rules."

Harper sensed a contradicting mixture of sincerity and deceit within Chase. His face—clean, steady, unperturbed—looked honest while his voice sounded deceitful.

She said, "We'll play here in the dining room and in the living room. You can use the restroom, you can get a drink from the kitchen, but you can't leave our sight. I don't want any of you exploring our cabin and messing around with anything. We're just going to play a friendly game. Is everyone okay with that?"

Dominic, Gina, Jackson, and Vanessa whispered amongst themselves. There was some uncertainty in the group, but they agreed to the terms. Brian crossed his arms and nodded at his wife—*okay, fine.*

Chase looked at Hazel and asked, "Are you okay with that, baby?"

"Sure," Hazel responded.

Chase glanced over at Rory and asked, "How about you? Can you follow the rules?"

Rory smiled and said, "No problem. I just need to use the restroom. I'm about to piss myself."

"It's right over there, buddy," Chase said as he pointed at the door in the dining room. He asked, "It's okay if he takes a piss, right, Harper?"

Harper said, "Yes. Yes, it's fine."

"Perfect."

Rory excused himself to the bathroom, carrying the bag with him. Brian thought: *what's in the bags? You planning on moving in or something?*

Breaking the silence, Gina said, "I guess we're playing another game. So, what's it going to be?"

Grinning, Chase responded, "How about charades?"

Chapter Seven

Charades

The group moved to the living room while Rory used the bathroom. Jackson sat on the recliner by himself. Brian, Harper, and Vanessa shared the three-seat sofa. And Dominic and Gina sat on the other couch. Chase and Hazel stood in front of them, standing between the coffee table and the entertainment center.

Chase said, "I'm going to be the... game master, so to speak. You can think of me as the referee, so I won't be playing with the rest of you. You can use Rory and Hazel as props, though. In fact, it's encouraged. It will add excitement to the game." He chuckled, then he said, "I mean, no offense, but some of you are hanging on the boring side of life. We'll change that tonight, though."

Hazel leered at Jackson and said, "Yes, we will." She looked at Brian, then at Dominic. She said, "I can't wait until we all play together. It's going to be... *magical.* Trust me, I'm a great player."

Vanessa sneered in disgust as Jackson chuckled with delight. Gina furrowed her brow as she analyzed Hazel's peculiar behavior. She couldn't tell if Hazel was genuinely trying to flirt with the men. Her intentions seemed sinister, despite her soft voice and playful words. Harper kept her eyes on Chase. He caught her interest, but she was no longer attracted to him.

Chase said, "We all know how to play charades. Two of you will come up here and act out the word or phrase I choose and the rest of you will have sixty seconds to try to guess that word or phrase. It could be a movie, a song, or just a word. We won't be breaking up into teams or anything like that, though. Instead, the game will end when you fail to identify a word."

"Fail?" Harper repeated, curious. She asked, "What happens if we fail?"

"Well, if you win three rounds, then you win the game—*bravo!* If you lose... then there will be consequences."

"We didn't agree to 'consequences,' Chase. We agreed to one quick game. That's it."

"It's okay. Relax. It won't be so bad anyway. Listen, you can't lose at something without there being consequences. That's not how life works. There may not be an answer to every question, but there are consequences to every action. If we ignored that tonight, we'd just be pretending to live. This is real, though. This is life."

The group shared the same thought: *what the hell is he talking about?* They were preparing to play a game of charades, but Chase was busy rambling about life and consequences. It sounded philosophical to them, but it didn't seem appropriate. Except for Jackson—always masculine and carefree—they were all confused and worried.

The muffled sound of a toilet flushing seeped into the room. The sound of running water followed. Then, the bathroom door swung open.

From the doorway, Rory said, "Much better. Much,

much better."

"Come over here, Rory. Join the party," Chase said as he beckoned to his friend. He turned his attention to the other guests and said, "I need a pen and some paper."

Brian sighed, then he said, "We have a magnetic notepad on the fridge. I'll get it for you. There are some pens on that table near the door. Help yourself."

While Brian went to the kitchen, Chase approached a console table behind the three-seat sofa. A tabletop picture frame contained a photograph of Brian and Harper. In the picture, Brian sat behind Harper, his arms wrapped around her body and his chin planted on her shoulder. They both smiled, but they didn't seem happy. Their eyes were so dull and hopeless. A stack of envelopes and a pen basket sat on the table, too.

Chase shook his head and rolled his eyes as he stared at the photograph. *Pictures tell a thousand lies,* he thought. He grabbed a pen, then he walked back to the space in front of the seating area. Brian handed him a small magnetic notepad—it was used for lists, but all of the sheets were blank. He returned to his seat, depressed and lethargic.

Chase said, "Alright, so that's everything I need. Let's get started."

***

Chase hummed and tapped the pen on the pad as he ran his eyes over the guests. He considered all of his options, hoping to maximize the fun. He wasn't interested in Brian and Dominic—not for that game, at least. The women didn't capture his attention, either. However, as soon as he spotted Jackson, his eyes lit up like a cat's eyes at night and a grin stretched from one side of his face to the other.

He said, "First up: Jackson and Hazel. Follow me and I'll give you your word."

Jackson asked, "Me? Really? I have to go first?"

Vanessa said, "Just get it over with, Jackson. I want this night to go back to normal already."

"Fine, whatever."

Chase pushed the picture frame aside and sat on the console table behind the sofa. He smirked as he jotted a note on the pad. Hazel hopped in place, unable to tame her excitement. Jackson dragged his feet to the couple. He didn't like Chase and he wasn't a fan of the game.

Rory leaned against the wall near the entertainment center, watching the other guests with a set of attentive eyes. His posture and demeanor resembled a prison guard's. Again, the group shared similar thoughts that boiled down to the same idea: *why is this stranger watching us like that?*

Chase showed the note to Jackson and Hazel. The note read: *A Serbian Film.* Jackson couldn't help but chuckle.

Chase asked, "You know it?"

Jackson responded, "I mean, yeah. Yeah, I know it. I don't know if they do, though."

"How about your girl?"

"Yeah, I watched it with her, but–"

"Then you have a chance to win. That's good enough. Now, go play the game."

Jackson reluctantly nodded in agreement. Hazel

patted his shoulder and nodded at the living room, as if to say: *showtime, let's play.* The pair made their way to the front of the seating area.

From the back of the room, Chase said, "I'm going to be counting in my head. You have sixty seconds. Your time... starts... *now.*"

Jackson glanced over at Hazel, hoping she would take the lead. To his dismay, Hazel just smirked and stared back at him. *It's a movie,* Jackson thought, *I should start with that.* He turned and faced the television, then he squatted and pretended to eat popcorn.

Dominic said, "Eating on the toilet."

Jackson shook his head—*no, not that.* He acted as if he were drinking from a straw, then he pretended to laugh. Hazel squatted beside him. She smiled as she reached into Jackson's invisible bag of popcorn. She scraped the crotch of his pants with her fingers. Jackson shuddered upon feeling her touch, but he didn't cause a scene.

Wide-eyed, Vanessa, unaware of Hazel's inappropriate behavior, shouted, "It's a movie!"

Jackson stood up, he pointed at his girlfriend, and he smiled and nodded—*exactly.* He thought: *now how do I explain that it's 'that' movie?*

Chase said, "Thirty-five seconds left."

Although reluctant, Jackson decided to pantomime Serbian stereotypes, hoping Vanessa would link the pieces. He had a sudden urge to win and he wouldn't let anything stop him, even if he acted offensively. He scowled and caressed his beard, then he pretended to drink while smoking a cigarette. He portrayed himself as a strong, stubborn man.

Dominic shrugged and asked, "What the hell is that supposed to be? Bad Santa?"

"Bad Santa 2?" Gina suggested.

Dominic looked at her and said, "We've been through this before: that movie doesn't exist."

"What are you talking about? We saw it in theaters together."

"That was just a bad dream. There's no way they would make a sequel like *that* to Bad Santa."

"Oh, come on, it wasn't that–"

"Twenty seconds," Chase interrupted. Speaking very slowly, he said, "Nine-teen sec-onds, eight-teen sec-onds..."

Hazel squatted with her knees spread wide. She grimaced in pain and panted, then she gasped. She reached for the area between her thighs, a motherly smile blossoming on her face. The audience understood her gestures: *childbirth.* Proud and joyful, the young woman was pretending to give birth while standing up.

Hazel acted as if she were cradling an infant in her arms for three measly seconds, then she held the invisible baby near Jackson's crotch. She nodded eagerly at him—*do it.*

Jackson recognized the scene. He didn't want to act it out, though. It was one of the most disturbing scenes in *A Serbian Film.* It was even considered to be one of the most disturbing scenes of all time. In the scene, Miloš, a semi-retired porn star, watched as a man helped a woman deliver a baby. Afterward, the man raped the infant in what the director called: *newborn porn.*

Jackson could separate reality from fiction. Hazel wasn't actually carrying an infant in her hands. Yet, the act still felt depraved.

Chase said, "You're running out of time. Do you want to lose so soon? Do you really want to suffer the consequences?"

Harper glanced over her shoulder and said, "We didn't agree to consequences, damn it."

"You did. You all did. Ten, nine, eight..."

Jackson groaned in exasperation. He shook his head and frowned at Vanessa as he thrust his hips at Hazel's hands. Hazel looked up at him, eyes glittering with deviance. It wasn't real, they were acting, but it still excited her.

While the rest of the group sneered in disgust and looked away, Vanessa shouted, "*A Serbian Film!* It's *A Serbian Film,* isn't it?"

"Ding, ding, ding," Chase said. "You are correct, Vanessa. You led your team to victory. I hope you're happy. If you end up losing, I'll make sure you're excused from the punishment."

"Punishment?" Harper repeated, a pinch of anger in her voice. She glared at Chase and asked, "What are you planning?"

"You'll see... or maybe you won't."

As Jackson returned to his seat, ashamed of himself, Vanessa said, "I can't believe you would pick *that* scene. You know I hated that part. It made me sick. It made me angry, Jackson. Why would you do that?"

Jackson responded, "I didn't pick it. You saw it yourself." He jabbed his index finger at Hazel and said, "This sick cunt picked it."

"Whoa!" Hazel shouted, pleasantly surprised. She smiled smugly and said, "So mean, so strong. You're a real tough guy, aren't you? I like that."

"Fuck off."

Chase clapped three times, stealing the spotlight and capturing their undivided attention. He said, "Let's stop fighting. We have a game to play, remember? So, next up is... Gina and Rory."

***

Gina held Dominic's hand and gazed into his eyes. She sought reassurance and security in her boyfriend—and she found it. Dominic's eyes said something along the lines of: *everything's okay, it's just a game.* She took a deep breath, then she walked back to Chase.

Rory nonchalantly dropped his bag on the floor beside the entertainment center. It landed with a loud *thump* and the impact even shook the floorboards. He joined Gina and Chase at the back of the room while Hazel took his place.

Gina asked, "What's our word?"

Chase showed them the notepad. The page read: *giving a blowjob.* Gina stared at the page with a deadpan expression, then she laughed.

Rory smiled and said, "It's easy, but it sounds like fun."

"I thought you'd like it," Chase responded.

Still laughing, Gina said, "Wait a minute. No, just... just wait a minute." She closed her eyes and shook her head, trying her best to calm herself. She said, "You can't be serious. This is... It's inappropriate. This is just wrong, guys. I'm not doing it."

Chase said, "If you don't do it, then you forfeit. If

you forfeit, you lose. If you lose, you'll be punished. Is that what you want?"

Without looking back, Harper said, "We did *not* agree to any punishments."

Brian muttered, "We shouldn't have agreed to anything at all."

Gina sensed the hostility in Chase's voice. She knew there was something wrong. However, at the same time, she sincerely believed the intruders would leave if they won the game.

She said, "Fine. I'll play along."

Gina and Rory walked to their stage. Gina giggled nervously as her friends looked back at her. Her cheeks turned pink, her eyes glistened with anxious tears. Stage fright crept up on her like a hospital bill —unexpected, *horrifying.* She had performed fellatio before, but she didn't openly talk about sex.

Chase said, "Your time starts now."

Gina bit her bottom lip and nodded. She had an idea. She opened her mouth—*aah!*—then she pushed her tongue against the side of her mouth. She moved her head back and forth, but she lost control of herself. She felt ridiculous as she sucked on an imaginary penis. She had to stop to laugh at the absurdity.

She said, "I'm sorry, I don't know what–"

"No talking," Chase said. "Forty, thirty-nine, thirty-eight."

Gina looked as if she were about to cry. Her left eye and the left side of her mouth twitched with embarrassment. *You know it,* she thought as she looked at her friends, *half of you have done it before, just say it so this can end already.* To her dismay, her friends didn't say a word. They knew about fellatio, but it didn't come to mind. It didn't seem like 'that' kind of game after all.

Rory grabbed Gina's shoulders. He turned her towards him, then he pushed down on her shoulders. Gina was a small, frail woman. She was also confused and afraid. So, it was easy to force her down to her knees. Rory smirked and nodded at her, as if to say: *go on, you know what to do.* Gina whimpered and shook her head, disgusted.

The truth finally dawned on the guests: *it was 'that' kind of game.*

Rory wound his fingers into her hair. Against her will, he pulled her head closer to him while thrusting his hips at her face. He tilted his head back like if he had a bloody nose—like if he was getting his dick sucked by a veteran porn star.

Chase said, "Ten seconds left."

Fists clenched, Dominic leaned forward in his seat and asked, "Is this some sort of sick joke? What the hell are you doing? Get your hands off of her!"

Brian stood from his seat and said, "Enough. The game is over. I want you all out of my house."

"Your time is up," Chase said. "You lost. You *actually* lost at charades. Well, I guess it's time for your punishment."

Jackson stood up and said, "The man said he wants you out of his house, so get the fuck out."

Rory unzipped his pants while the group argued with Chase. Gina's eyes widened as Rory's semi-erect penis and scrotum flopped out of his fly. Rory lunged forward and swung his genitals at Gina's face. His penis hit her right eye and his scrotum scraped her nose. She even felt some of his pubic hairs caress her lips.

Gina fell back and shrieked. She crawled backwards until the back of her head hit the wall under a window.

Upon spotting his genitals, Dominic shouted, "You sick bastard!"

He rushed forward and shoved Rory with all of his might. Rory laughed as he crashed into the television mounted on the wall. Then, Jackson lunged forward and hit him twice—a right hook followed by a left uppercut. Dazed by the blows, Rory stopped laughing. He wrapped his arms around his head and staggered away from them.

Chase shouted, "I said time's up! You lose!"

Brian said, "I've had enough of this game. We want you to leave."

"Leave?" Dominic repeated as he crouched beside Gina. He shouted, "I want them arrested, Brian! That punk assaulted Gina!"

Chase said, "Listen, Rory took things a little too far, but that doesn't change the rules of the game. You lost, so you owe us another one."

Harper grabbed her cell phone from the neighboring end table. She rubbed her forehead with her fingertips and said, "Party's over. I'm calling the cops."

Chase said, "Call the cops, your families, your friends... Call everyone. It won't change a thing. We won't leave until the game is over. You lost—*again*—so you owe us another game. That is the consequence of failure. It's going to get worse than that, though, especially if you keep acting up. This was the... the warm-up round. You don't want to lose the next few games."

Harper and Vanessa ignored his speech. They tapped and swiped at their cell phones, frantically trying to call the police, but their calls wouldn't connect. They couldn't send text messages, either. Dominic and Gina sat in the corner of the room. Gina sobbed into Dominic's chest, traumatized by the assault. Meanwhile, Jackson and Brian inched closer to Chase.

Before anyone could make a move, Harper said, "I don't have signal. I mean, there's no reception at all. I can't call anyone, Brian."

"I can't, either," Vanessa said, her voice shaking with fear. "What's going on? I was just texting earlier."

Brian said, "That's impossible. You should at least be able to call emergency services. This is prime real estate. Let me–"

"It's them," Jackson interrupted, his sharp eyes locked on Chase. All of their eyes drifted towards him. Jackson continued, "You're messing with us, aren't you? This is all part of your little game, huh? You little punk..."

Jackson launched himself forward. He swung at Chase. His right hook barely touched Chase's chin, his knuckles gliding across his skin. Chase wrapped his arms around his head and leaned back. He ate Jackson's punches like a trained boxer. He felt some pain across his arms and abdomen, but he refused to fall.

"Jackson, watch out!" Vanessa shouted as she watched the action from the sofa.

Hazel shot a stun gun at Jackson. The prongs penetrated the small of his back. The hulking man gritted his teeth and hissed as his limbs stiffened. A jolt of electricity surged across his body. Stiff like a tree, he fell to his side. The side of his head hit the edge of the table, then he landed on the floor— temporarily paralyzed and unconscious.

Hazel whispered, "Timber."

Vanessa fell to her knees beside Jackson. She shook his shoulders and cried, begging him to wake up. Brian leaned on the sofa near his wife, lightheaded, while Harper stared down at Jackson in utter awe. They were both stunned by the event. While Gina cowered in the corner, Dominic ran forward. *Tackle Hazel,* he thought, *take the Taser and gain the upper hand.*

Before he could reach her, Chase and Rory drew pistols from the back of their waistbands. Chase pulled Hazel behind him and aimed the compact gun at Dominic's head, stopping him in his tracks. Rory stayed near the entertainment center, aiming his pistol at the rest of the group. At such a close range, it was too risky for them to try to run.

Dominic raised his hands over his head and said, "Take it easy, man. We don't want any trouble. We just want you to leave. That's all. We'll... We'll let bygones be bygones."

Chase said, "Take a seat. Go on, take a seat."

Rory aimed his gun at Gina and said, "You too. Get up and get back to your seat."

Dominic walked back to Gina's side. He moved slowly in hopes of defusing the tension. He grabbed her waist in one hand and her left hand in the other.

Sniveling and muttering, they reluctantly returned to the two-seat sofa. Brian raised his hands and walked backwards. He nodded at Rory as he sat down beside his wife—*I'm cool, everything's okay.*

Harper leaned closer to Brian and, in a shaky voice, she whispered, "What are we going to do?"

Avoiding eye contact, Brian responded, "I don't know."

"You don't know? We're in trouble, Brian. This is serious. They... They have guns."

"I know. I can see that. I just... I don't know, okay? I don't know."

Harper stared down at her baby bump and whispered, "Oh, God, what have we done? We're all dead, aren't we? This can't be happening. It's a dream. It's a bad dream..."

Chase said, "Go back to your seat, Vanessa."

Vanessa shook her head and cried, "He's hurt! He needs help!"

"Go back to your seat or I'll put a bullet in the back of his head. Do you want that to happen? Do you want me to kill this animal?"

"He's not a damn animal! He's my boyfriend! You can't do this to us!"

"He's an animal and he started this. Go back to your seat or he dies."

Vanessa looked up at Chase, then down at Jackson, and then back at Chase. She felt the sincerity in Chase's voice—his threat was genuine. She kissed the nape of Jackson's neck, she whispered some words of reassurance into his ear, then she returned to her seat beside Harper.

Chase said, "Hazel, get your gun out and watch

them. We're going to restrain this *beast* before he tries anything else."

"Sure thing, babe," Hazel responded.

Hazel pulled a six-round revolver out of her backpack. She stood in front of the television and, holding it with both hands, she aimed the revolver at the group. Her finger rested on the trigger—ready, *eager.* The side of her mouth rose in a smirk of deviance. She wanted to kill them. The thought of murder aroused her.

Each of them gripping one arm, Chase and Rory lifted Jackson from the floor. They threw him onto the recliner. Rory pulled a bloody jump rope out of his duffel bag. He tied the rope around Jackson's body and the chair, restraining him to the recliner. Chase duct-taped Jackson's arms to the armrests— from his wrists to the crooks of his elbows.

The other guests spotted the blood on the jump rope. Two questions emerged in their minds: *why do they have jump rope? And, why is there blood on that rope?* They believed the intruders stole the jump rope after hurting another group. The idea terrified them because it meant the intruders were experienced. It wasn't their first rodeo.

As he added a fifth layer of tape to Jackson's arms, Chase said, "We won't restrain the rest of you as long as you cooperate. It wouldn't be fun if you were all tied up. And, that's what this night is all about: *fun.*" He patted Jackson's arms, ensuring the tape was secured, then he approached the entertainment center. He smiled and said, "You can try to run, you can even try to fight us, but it won't end well for you. There's only three of us and six of you, but, at such close quarters, I'm positive we'd at least shoot two of you before you even touched any of us."

Rory jabbed his gun at the back of Jackson's head. He said, "And even if all of you got away, this asshole would still be with us. We could hurt him for a long time before you could get help. I know some of you actually care about him, so you don't want to leave him in our hands. Don't be stupid."

Vanessa held her hand over her forehead and sobbed. She wheezed and snorted. Her boyfriend was alive, but the mere thought of his potential death devastated her. Harper pulled Vanessa closer to her chest, coddling her like a baby. She kissed her head and caressed her hair.

Chase said, "If you cooperate, all of you will have the opportunity to survive. It's that simple, I swear."

Dominic asked, "What the hell do you want from us?"

"We just want to finish our game."

Chapter Eight

The Game, The Rules

A wave of tension descended upon the group—
gripping them, *smothering them.* The party-goers,
defenseless and helpless, were held hostage at
gunpoint by a group of armed thugs. Their thoughts
were split into two separate categories. Dominic,
Gina, and Brian thought about survival while
Vanessa and Harper thought about death. Jackson
was barely awakening, eyes flickering and lips
fluttering.

Chase said, "I want to be honest with you.
Transparent, you know? So, here's what's going to
happen. We're going to have fun tonight. We're going
to play some of our favorite party games until five in
the morning, around the time the sun rises. Each
time you lose a game, you will be punished. If you
win a game... Well, we don't have any prizes, but we
can reward you with nothing. You heard that right:
nothing. It doesn't sound like much of a prize, but,
compared to the punishments we have planned...
Let's just say 'nothing' is better than something."

"Oh, God," Gina cried. She tightened her grip on
her boyfriend's hand. She repeated, "Oh, God."

Dominic stared vacantly at his hand, then at his
lap. He was trapped in a fear-induced trance. He
couldn't stop his leg from shaking. He didn't know
Chase's plans, but he was still scared. The ominous
secrecy—the inability to predict his inevitable

torture—terrified him more than anything else at the moment.

Chase continued, "There is a bright side, though —a silver lining. We're going to punish you after each loss, but that doesn't mean you're going to die. Hell, even if you were hurt after each game, you might survive if you're strong and resilient." He chuckled, then he said, "You might be missing a few pieces of your bodies in the end, but at least you'll be alive, right? Isn't that all that matters to people? We all just want to live, don't we?"

The group burst into a discordant symphony of whining, begging, and screaming. *Missing a few pieces*—those words told them that they were going to be brutally tortured. Dismemberment was supposed to happen in accidents, it was supposed to occur in videos on the internet, but it wasn't supposed to happen to them.

Brian said, "We'll pay you. I have cash in my bedroom. It's not much, we just keep it in case of emergencies, but I think it's enough for all of you. You can take our jewelry, our clothes, my credit cards, my car... You can take it all and you can disappear. No one has to know that this happened. It can still go away. Okay? Alright?"

Chase stared at Brian with a steady expression. He tilted his head, like a dog hearing a peculiar noise for the first time. Without taking his eyes off of Brian, he stepped forward until his knees touched the edge of the table, then he leaned forward.

He asked, "Was that a serious offer?"

"Y–Yes. Take it all."

"Brian, do you try to solve all of your problems

with money? Hmm? Are you the type of person who assumes every problem is caused by money—too much, too little, or none at all?"

"No. No, I'm not. I'm just trying to think logically. This is a... a home invasion, isn't it? We're being held at gunpoint for a reason and the most common reason for home invasions is burglary. So, I'm giving you what you want on a silver platter."

"No. You're giving me what you *think* I want. We don't want your money. Haven't you been listening? We want to have fun."

"We want to party," Hazel said as she walked behind the two-seat sofa, aiming the revolver at Gina and Dominic.

Brian said, "You can have plenty of fun with our money. You can rent your own cabin, you can buy booze and drugs, you can hire some escorts or strippers, you can do whatever you want. We just want this to end in peace. Okay? Please don't take this any further. *Please.*"

Chase snickered, then he asked, "Is that what you do with your money, Brian? You rent cabins, you buy drugs, and you order hookers?" He looked at Harper and asked, "Is that why your relationship is on the rocks?"

Harper looked away from Chase and said, "You bastard, you sick bastard..."

"I'm right, aren't I? Goddamn it, you're all so pathetic. Selfish, greedy, two-faced."

Brian ran his hand over his face and rubbed his eyes. Harper and Vanessa continued to sob in each other's arms. Dominic and Gina watched the confrontation from the sidelines, speechless.

Judging from their reactions, there was obviously some truth in Chase's theory.

Chase took three steps back. He said, "I sensed the... the *negative* energy as soon as I walked in here. A bad aura, you know? Now I understand why your so-called 'friends' are more like enemies, Brian. You're a pretentious little prick who thinks too highly of himself, but these cunts tolerate you so they can benefit from your wealth." Pacing back and forth in front of the coffee table, he said, "You know, you remind me of a celebrity, but not in a good way. I'm not saying your handsome or charismatic or talented. I'm saying you're disconnected from reality. You don't understand your 'friends' or their struggles, but you still pretend to 'get it.' You pretend to know an everyday person's struggles while vacationing at a lake house that you *own*. You're the type of man to tell a depressed person: 'try not being depressed.' You just don't get it and you never will."

Brian leaned on the armrest and kept his hand over his face. He couldn't stop himself from crying. *You're right, I don't get it,* he thought, *I don't know what to do, I never know what to do.*

Chase looked at the rest of the group and said, "Now that we're past that... Are we ready to play?"

There was no response, just sniveling and murmuring. They weren't interested in Chase's brand of 'fun.' They didn't have any other options, though.

Hazel tapped the barrel of her gun on Dominic's head, causing him to bounce on his seat. She asked, "What do you want to play first, baby?"

Dominic leaned closer to Gina and glanced over his shoulder. He glared at Hazel, sending a stern message with his fierce eyes: *don't touch me again.* Hazel wasn't intimidated by Dominic's glare, though. She had a revolver after all. She giggled and aimed the gun at Gina's head.

The young woman asked, "What do you want to play, sweetie?"

Gina looked at Hazel for a second—*just a second*—then she whimpered and buried her face in Dominic's chest. She was afraid of Hazel, although the woman was petite, peppy, and pretty.

Chase said, "They don't want to choose, so I will. Let's start with... the ice cube melting game. Have any of you played it before?" Yet again, the group did not respond. Chase said, "Well, let me tell you how it works. You'll be split into two pairs and each pair will have a captain. The captain will not be allowed to play, though. Each pair will be given a bowl of ice cubes. The goal is to melt all of the ice without using your mouths. The captain of the losing team will be punished. Understood?"

Through his gritted teeth, Jackson muttered, "You little punks..." He tried to lean forward, but the rope and tape kept him restrained to the recliner. He shouted, "You can't do this! You can't 'punish' us for playing a game we don't even want to play in the first place! You can't do that! It's crazy!"

"We're not punishing you for playing. We're punishing you for *losing.* There's a lack of responsibility... Scratch that, there's a *severe* lack of responsibility in today's world. People, especially 'elites' like Brian, aren't punished for their actions and that's just wrong. This game is going to teach you about teamwork and consequences. It's going to teach you about friends and failures. But, most importantly, it's going to show you how to have fun."

"Yeah!" Hazel said enthusiastically. "Let's do it. Let's have some fun already."

"You heard the lady," Chase said. He nodded at Rory and said, "I can watch them. Go to the kitchen. Grab two bowls and check if they have ice in the freezer. If they don't, we'll have to ask a neighbor or something. Or, we'll just have to punish all of them for being bad hosts. A party without ice? Now that's just crazy."

Rory walked to the kitchen, aiming his pistol at the guests each step of the way. In the kitchen, he opened the freezer. He found three ten-pound bags of ice stacked on top of each other.

He yelled, "They have plenty, Chase! Looks like they were going to have a wild party with some cold drinks! I guess they're not bad hosts after all!"

Chapter Nine

The Ice Cube Race

A porcelain soup bowl sat at each end of the coffee table. Plumes of water vapor rose from the mounds of ice cubes in the bowls. Hazel stood behind the two-seat sofa, Rory sat on the console table at the back of the room, and Chase remained in front of the entertainment center. The preparations were complete.

Chase said, "Since Jackson can't play, he'll be the captain of Team One. So, who wants to be on Team One?"

Vanessa immediately raised her hand, determination written on her face. She was ready to fight for Jackson's safety. The rest of the group wasn't as eager, though. If they failed, they didn't want to be responsible for someone else's pain.

Chase said, "Okay. Vanessa and Brian will be on Team One. Dominic, you'll be the captain of Team Two, which will consist of Harper and Gina. The rest of us won't be playing in this game since we have to make sure you don't do anything stupid, but enough talking. Let's start this before the ice melts on its own. You have sixty seconds to melt as much ice as possible. Ready, set, *go.*"

Gina and Harper glanced at each other with a look that said: *oh, God, this is really happening.* The women bolted into action. Vanessa grabbed Brian's wrist and pulled him off the sofa. She fell to her knees between the coffee table and the recliner.

As she grabbed a handful of ice, Vanessa said, "Don't worry, baby. We're going to save you."

Vanessa rubbed the ice between her palms, then she exhaled onto the chunk. The ice slipped and slid in her hands like a bar of soap in the shower, but she held onto it. She felt the cold water streaming down her forearms as the ice melted slowly.

She blew on the ice, then she shouted, "Hurry, Brian!"

Brian grabbed a chunk of ice—four, maybe five ice cubes stuck together. He wrapped his shirt around the ice and pressed down on it. *Is this even doing anything?*–he thought.

Vanessa nudged Brian's arm and said, "Blow on it. You're not melting it fast enough."

"I'm doing my best," Brian said, his shirt soaked with cold water. He pulled the ice away from his shirt and said, "We need to try something else."

"I said blow on it!"

"That's not working! We need to do something else, damn it!"

Jackson shouted, "Hey! Watch your mouth before I knock your teeth out, punk!"

Brian looked back at Jackson and snapped, "I'm on your side! I'm playing to save you!"

"Then listen to her!"

Chase chuckled, then he said, "Thirty seconds left."

Harper and Gina started the game with the same strategy: blowing on the ice and applying pressure to the cubes. Their results were similar, so the race was close.

Dominic leaned closer to them and, in a low tone to avoid being heard by the other team, he said, "Rub it between your bodies, between your chests. It should be warmer than your hands."

Although hesitant, Harper and Gina were determined to win. Gina raised her sweatshirt up to her neck, revealing her bare abdomen and bra. Harper tugged on the collar of her house-dress until her bra was visible. They leaned closer together, then they placed a chunk of ice between their breasts. They couldn't help but gasp and shudder upon feeling the cold, wet ice.

The cool temperature caused the hairs at the back of their necks to prickle. It didn't stop them, though. They cocked their heads back and blew down on the cubes, too. To their pleasant surprise, the ice actually melted faster than before. They pulled ahead in the race, leaving Vanessa and Brian in the dust.

Chase licked his lips as he watched the icy water coursing down to Gina's belly button. He was attracted to her. He was dating Hazel, but she didn't mind anyway. She was attracted to Gina, too.

Chase said, "Five, four, three, two... *one!* Game's over! Drop the ice and get back to your seats."

The ice cubes *clinked* and *clunked* as they fell on the floor and table. Gina dried her torso with her sweater, then she put on her jacket as she returned to her seat. Harper crossed her arms and rubbed her shoulders as she sat down on the three-seat sofa. Brian and Vanessa looked at each other with resentment in their eyes as they sat down. They weren't as cold as the others since they didn't use the same tactics.

Chase approached the bowl in front of Dominic. He examined the ice as well as the water on the floor and in the bowl. He puckered his lips and shrugged —*interesting.* He looked at the other bowl and examined the area under Jackson's feet. He scoffed, unimpressed by the puddle. He returned to his position in front of the television, smiling smugly.

He said, "The winner is... Team Two."

Gina let out a loud sigh of relief while Dominic smiled and looked up at the ceiling. Jackson shuddered in his seat, although he fought to hide his fear.

Vanessa said, "I'm sorry, baby. I'm so sorry."

"It's not your fault, so don't apologize to me," Jackson said. He glared at Chase as his breathing intensified. He said, "This is *their* fault. They're trying to hurt us, they're trying to break us apart. They're responsible for this. Not you, Vanessa."

Chase responded, "I like the way you think, Jack. I still think Vanessa and Brian share some responsibility, but you're partially correct. We're hurting you, so we're responsible for your pain. It's that simple, isn't it? You're practical, you're smart. That's not going to get you out of this, though." He glanced over at Rory and said, "Find two buckets and fill 'em up with the coldest water you can get. Bring a bag of ice out here, too."

＊＊＊

Rory entered the room through the kitchen door, carrying a plastic bucket in each hand. The sound of splashing water emerged from the containers. He placed the buckets in front of the recliner, then he drew his handgun and returned to his position behind the three-seat sofa. He aimed the gun at the hostages, ready to shoot at the first sign of trouble.

Chase beckoned to Hazel and said, "You know the plan, babe. Get going."

"*Finally,*" Hazel said excitedly. "I've been waiting all night for this."

She handed her revolver to Chase, then she knelt down in front of Jackson. She removed his boots and socks, then she rolled his pants up to his knees, despite his resistance.

Chase aimed the pistol at the two-seat sofa and the revolver at Jackson. His pose made him feel giddy. He felt like the star of an action movie.

As she lifted his left foot, Hazel said, "Don't kick me and don't knock over these buckets. If you do that... Let's see..." She giggled, then she said, "If you do that, I'll give you a urethra paper-cut."

Jackson cringed as he thought about having his urethra *sliced* with a sheet of paper. He thought: *what the fuck? What is wrong with these people?* He couldn't conjure the words to respond.

Hazel put his left foot in one of the buckets. She did the same to his right foot. The buckets reached up to the center of his shins. The buckets were filled halfway with cold water—around forty-five degrees Fahrenheit.

Jackson felt uncomfortable, but the cold water didn't hurt him. In fact, the water actually helped him get his mind off of Hazel's disgusting threat.

He chuckled, then he asked, "This is it? This is your punishment? Holy shit, I actually thought you were going to hurt me. This... This is nothing compared to the shit they put in movies these days. This is a day at the spa for a guy like me."

Hazel tapped his shins and said, "Hey, if you'd like me to cut your dick with paper, feel free to knock over one of these buckets. That offer is still on the table, big guy"

"Stop saying that."

"Then stop trying to poke my buttons. I'm not a video game, you know?"

"Yeah? Well, I thought you wanted to have fun."

As she lifted the heavy bag of ice from the floor, Hazel said, "Oh, I'm going to have *a lot* of fun with you. This is only the beginning."

The young woman dumped ice into each bucket. The ice buried Jackson's feet and swallowed his legs up to his shins. Rivers of cold water flowed between the cubes. Jackson grimaced and squirmed on his seat. The ice burned his skin, creating a stinging sensation across his feet and ankles. After a minute, he began to feel a tingling sensation in his toes.

Vanessa stuttered, "Wha–What are you doing to him? You... You're going to freeze his feet like that. He'll get... He'll get frostbite, won't he?" She looked at Harper, then at Brian. She repeated, "He'll get frostbite, won't he?"

Chase said, "I guess it's possible. If that happens, we'll just have to amputate his feet."

"No, please don't do this," Vanessa cried.

"What's the matter? You'd still love him even if he didn't have a foot to stand on, right?"

Vanessa stood up.

Before she could take a step, Rory said, "You move, you die. Don't test me."

Vanessa glanced over at Rory, then she looked back at Jackson. She scrunched up her face and shook her head. She didn't know what to do, but she felt like she had to do something.

His voice trembling, Jackson stuttered, "S–Sit dow–down, Vanessa. I–I'm... I'm okay." He cracked a smile—a forced smile—and said, "This is nothing. This is... nothing."

Vanessa reluctantly sat down. Harper attempted to comfort her, but to no avail. Brian, Dominic, and Gina didn't say a word, dumbstruck by the bizarre torture.

Chase said, "Get away from him, Hazel." Kittenish, Hazel giggled as she took her revolver back and returned to her position. Chase said, "Jackson, you sit still and we'll come back to you after the next game. The sooner we get started, the sooner your punishment can end. Okay?"

Jackson responded, "J–Just hurry up already."

"Of course, captain. Let's get this show on the road."

Chapter Ten

Truth or Dare

Chase said, "I want to play something simple while we allow Jackson's feet to get 'nice and cold.' You know, I want to play something that doesn't require a lot of work. It has to be fun, though. It's not a game if it's not fun, right? Any suggestions? Hmm?"

The hostages remained quiet, teary-eyed and stony-faced. They didn't even spare a glance for the demented young man.

Chase said, "Okay, alright. I'll choose for you. Let's see... Let's see..." His eyes widened, his brow rose, and his lips curled with delight. He said, "Truth or dare.... Truth or dare, also known as 'questions and demands' during certain periods in history, is a well-known party game. Everyone's played it and, if you haven't, you're a lying son of a bitch who deserves a bullet between the eyes."

Dominic muttered to himself, Gina and Brian stayed quiet, and Harper and Vanessa whimpered. None of them were amused by the playful threat of violence.

Chase said, "Relax, guys. I'm just messing with you. A bullet to the head would be too easy."

"Just get to your damn point already," Jackson snapped, shivering with the cold.

"I'm getting there. What was I saying? Oh, truth or dare. We're playing truth or dare, okay? The rules will be slightly different, though. Since I don't want you all to choose 'truth,' that wouldn't be any fun, we're going to choose through the flip of a coin. Heads will mean 'truth,' tails will mean 'dare. If you refuse your dare or if you lie to me, you will be punished. Got that?"

Harper asked, "How would you know if we're lying to you? Are you a psychic or something?"

"More like a psycho," Jackson muttered.

Chase pulled a steel claw hammer out of Hazel's backpack. He shoved the pistol into the back of his waistband, then he swung the hammer through the air—*whoosh.*

He said, "You better make me believe you or I'm going to make you feel a lot of pain." He pulled a quarter out of his pocket and said, "We'll start with Dominic, the brilliant-but-tired writer."

He approached the coffee table and stared down at Dominic. Dominic stared back at him, fighting the urge to attack him. *They'd actually shoot me,* he thought, *but what if their guns aren't loaded?* He couldn't take the risk.

Chase flipped the coin, he caught it in his left hand, then he slapped it onto the top of his right hand. *Tails.*

He said, "It looks like you get a dare, Dominic. I dare you to... headbutt your girlfriend."

"What? No, I'm not doing that."

"You're not doing it? You got tails, man. You have to do it. It's the rules."

"I'm not headbutting her."

Chase placed the hammer on the coffee table, then he drew his pistol. He placed the muzzle of the gun on Dominic's thigh. Dominic leaned back in his seat and gasped upon feeling the gun. Gina imagined herself grabbing the hammer and crushing Chase's head with it, but she was paralyzed by her fear. *Damn it, damn it, damn it,* she thought, *why can't I do anything to help him?*

Chase said, "If you don't do it, I'll shoot your leg. I won't even aim, I'll just shoot. You don't want that to happen. I could hit an artery, right? And, if that happened, there would be no way for any of us to stop the bleeding. So, you'd die. That's exciting, but I don't want to lose a player so early in the game. So, are you going to follow the rules? Or are you going to keep acting like a little bitch?"

Gina said, "Do it, Dom. Just do it."

Dominic sighed in disappointment. He turned in his seat and faced his girlfriend. He saw the fear and pain in her eyes. He cocked his head back, then he thrust it forward. He slowed down before hitting her, though. His forehead collided with her chin—*thud.*

Gina held her hand over her mouth. She felt slight pain across her chin, a bruise would surely materialize in a day or two, but she would survive.

Chase asked, "What the hell was that?"

Dominic responded, "I did what you told me to do."

"You think this is a joke, don't you? I told you to headbutt her, I didn't tell you to tap her with your forehead. Headbutt her! Headbutt her or I'm going to shoot one of your balls off! I'll do it, man! I really will!"

"Wait, wait, wait!" Gina cried, holding her hand up to Chase in a peaceful gesture. She looked at

Dominic and said, "Headbutt me. I can take it."

Dominic closed his eyes, causing rivers of tears to course down his cheeks. He looked at Gina once more, his eyes pleading for forgiveness. He cocked his head back, then he thrust it forward with all of his might—*thud!*

They fell away from each other, dazed by the collision. Gina nearly fell off the sofa. She kept her balance by grabbing onto the back cushion of the sofa. Blood oozed out of her gums and flooded her mouth. A gooey string of blood dripped from the side of her mouth and fell to the floor. Her bottom teeth felt loose, as if they would pop out at any moment.

There was a red mark on Dominic's forehead. His skin wasn't cut, but he suffered from a massive headache.

Stunned, he leaned closer to her and stuttered, "I–I'm sorry. I'm sorry, sweetie."

"It's okay. I'm... I'm okay."

Chase, Hazel, and Rory laughed during the entire encounter. They were amused by the simple things in life—party games, home invasions, *torture.*

Chase said, "Okay, okay. That's enough of that. You passed. Let's move on to Gina." He took two steps to his right and stopped in front of her. He asked, "You ready to play, Gina? Hmm? You still with us?"

Gina wiped the tears from her eyes, then she swiped at the blood dripping from her lip. Without making eye contact, she nodded at Chase—*I'm ready, let's get it over with.* Chase flipped the coin, he caught it, then he slapped it onto his hand.

He said, "Heads."

"Too bad," Hazel said. "The game was just getting good."

"Don't worry, babe. An honest conversation can be just as fun as a violent thrill ride," Chase responded. He gazed into Gina's eyes and said, "Tell me, Gina: if one of you had to die tonight for this nightmare to end, who would you pick and why?"

Gina grimaced as she loudly swallowed. The pungent taste of blood overwhelmed her. She was still dazed by the headbutt, but she understood the question. She didn't want to answer it, though. She could see Chase was trying to physically and psychologically torture them.

She said, "I, um... I don't know."

"You don't know? Well, you can start by crossing yourself off that list. I barely met you, but I already know you're not the type to sacrifice yourself. Your relationship might not be perfect, but you wouldn't kill Dominic, either, so you can take him off the list, too. That leaves the rest of them. Who would you have us kill to end this horrible night?"

"I told you: I don't know. Please, don't make me do this."

Rory jabbed his pistol at the back of Harper's head. He said, "Maybe we should pick for her. Maybe we should actually do it, too."

Harper and Vanessa cried in each other's arms while Brian leaned away from them.

Jackson stuttered, "P–Pick anyone, Gina. We... We know you don't mean it. F–Fuck these guys."

Chase said, "Don't listen to him. You have to be honest, remember? So, who's it going to be? You have ten seconds to choose, then... then things start getting violent. Ten, nine, eight..."

Gina blinked rapidly as she looked at her friends. Her vision was blurred due to the tears in her eyes, but she could still see the fear on their faces.

As Chase's countdown reached three, Gina closed her eyes and shouted, "Brian! I choose Brian!"

The intruders *oohed* and *aahed* like teenagers watching a classmate argue with a teacher. All of their eyes wandered to Brian, eager to see his reaction.

Brian shrugged and said, "Whatever. It's fine. It's okay, Gina."

Hazel said, "Your 'friend' wants you dead and you're okay with that?"

"I don't care, really."

Chase said, "Good choice, Gina. I believe you, but I still need to know why. Why would you have him killed?"

"Because... Because he's wealthy, he's successful, and he's... he's a snob. He won't admit it, but he thinks he's better than the rest of us. He acts like a... a saint, but he has just as many demons in him as the rest of us. That's why. Okay? Are you happy now?"

Chase responded, "You're pathetic, Gina, but I get it. A lot of people think like you nowadays. They're jealous of others and they let that jealousy consume their lives. They would let someone die just because they're so bitter and envious. It's insane, isn't it? At least your honest, though—honest and resentful."

Ashamed and afraid, Gina could only cry. She kept her head down, refusing to look at her friends. She certainly didn't want to meet eyes with Brian.

Shaking and panting, Jackson said, "I... I can't feel my feet. Can you... Can you get my feet out of the buckets? Please?"

Chase beckoned to Hazel and said, "Do your thing."

Hazel skipped happily to the recliner. Instead of pulling Jackson's feet out, she dumped more ice into the buckets. Icy water overflowed from the buckets and spilled onto the floorboards.

Jackson cried, "Goddammit!"

"You're hurting him," Vanessa said.

Chase grabbed her chin and turned her away from the recliner, forcing her to make eye contact with him. He said, "It's your turn. Remember, the sooner we finish this, the sooner we can get his feet out of those buckets. You ready to play?"

"Yes. Flip the coin. *Hurry.*"

"Sure, sure."

Chase flipped the coin. It landed on tails. He smirked as he glanced around the room, searching for the perfect dare. His eyes were naturally drawn to the buckets.

He said, "There's enough room in those buckets for a little more ice. I dare you to fill 'em up."

"No!" Vanessa yelled. She waved her arms like an umpire and said, "I'm not doing it. I *can't* do it."

"Come on, Vanessa. Don't make this hard for us."

"You're making this hard for me! I won't do it, damn it!"

"I'm getting tired of this cycle. You say, 'No, I'm not doing it,' then I say, 'I'm going to shoot you if you don't,' and then you end up doing it. It's boring, isn't it?"

"I don't care."

Jackson said, "Vanessa, don't fight them. It can't... It can't get any worse for me. Do it and move on."

Vanessa responded, "You'll lose your feet, baby. I can't let that happen to you. This is sick. I'm not playing."

Chase sternly said, "You're breaking the rules. I *will* punish you."

"Do it! Do some–"

Mid-sentence, Chase shot at Vanessa's leg. The bullet penetrated the center of her thigh and became lodged in her muscle. A geyser of blood gushed out of the wound. Vanessa quickly covered the gunshot wound, but to no avail. More blood oozed out from between her fingers and streamed across her shaking leg. She rocked back-and-forth and cried hysterically.

As she pushed herself to the edge of the seat, Harper yelled, "Oh my God!"

Brian wrapped his arms around his head and tucked himself into a ball, fearing he would be next. Gina covered her ears, closed her eyes, and cried. Jackson bounced on his seat and screamed at Chase, but his words were incomprehensible. The jump rope groaned as it nearly snapped. Dominic let out a piercing scream as he rushed forward. He tried to tackle Chase, but, before he could reach him, Rory struck the back of his head with the butt of his pistol.

Dominic fell to his knees in front of Chase. He didn't get the chance to fight back, though. He barely caught a glimpse of the hammer as Chase swung it at him. A dull *thud* accompanied the screaming and crying as the hammer hit the side of Dominic's head. Once again dazed by the blows to the head, Dominic's head spun. He struggled to his feet, then he teetered left-and-right like a drunk after a night at a bar.

Aiming the gun at the hostages, Hazel shouted, "Shut up! Shut the hell up!"

The noise slowly dwindled. Jackson still hurled insults at Chase while attempting to comfort his girlfriend with words of reassurance. Vanessa continued crying and panting. Dominic fell back into his seat where Gina examined his injuries and kissed his cheek. The entire group was terrified—and rightfully so. They shared another thought: *oh, God, the guns are real.*

As Chase aimed the pistol down at her, Vanessa stammered, "Do–Do–Don't sh–shoot. I don't... I don't want to die."

Chase said, "I'm not going to kill you, but I hope the rest of you understand that we're not messing around. We're playing party games, but don't play with us. Hazel, get a cloth and cover her leg. Make sure she doesn't bleed out. The rest of us are going to continue the game."

Hazel was happy to follow Chase's directions. She pulled a white t-shirt out of the duffel bag. She cut the shirt in half, then she tied the cloth around Vanessa's thigh—a makeshift bandage. The torn cloth was quickly soaked in blood, but the bleeding eventually slowed.

Chase flipped the coin in front of Brian. It landed on tails, but he wanted to have some fun with him. He was tired of dares anyway.

He said, "Heads. You got heads. Tell me, Brian, why did you *really* invite these people to this cabin?"

Brian sniffled as he looked at all of his friends. He couldn't stop his face from twitching. Anxiety and fear flowed through his veins like venom from a snake.

Tears welling in his eyes, he said, "I missed my friends. I missed being around... normal people. I've made some mistakes in my life, I've acted arrogant and stupid, but I've tried my best to change. I wanted to–to show that and... and I wanted to patch things up before I became a father. That's all."

Chase asked, "Is that your final answer."

"Y–Yes."

Pausing between each word, Chase said, "I... don't... believe... you."

He swiftly grabbed the hammer from the coffee table. He swung the hammer at Brian's face. The hammer hit his mouth, cutting his lips and chipping a tooth. A jolt of pain surged from his damaged tooth, reverberating across his gums. One hit wasn't enough, though. So, he swung it at his face *nine* more times.

Brian's chin was split down the middle vertically. Blood leaked from the wide gash, covering most of his neck and dripping down to his chest. One of his front incisor teeth was dislodged. The tooth swam in a pool of blood and saliva in his mouth. Then the tooth rode that wave of blood down his throat. His swollen gums and chipped, cracked teeth were painted red with blood.

He grimaced and screamed as he felt a pulsating pain across his gums. The stinging pain grew stronger with each throb.

His 'friends' watched the beating, but they didn't bother to help him. Disappointed in themselves, they sat quietly and listened to the *thudding* of the hammer as well as Brian's whimpers.

After the tenth hit, Chase tossed the bloody hammer on the coffee table and stepped away from Brian. He ran his fingers through his hair, leaving his beach blonde locks streaked with blood. He smiled as he watched Brian cover his face with his trembling hands. The sight of a grown man crying delighted him.

He said, "I hope you're all starting to get the idea. I don't *want* to hurt you, but I won't hesitate to punish you, either." He stared down at Harper and said, "It's your turn, Harper. Set an example for the rest of your friends, okay?"

Harper nodded reluctantly. She didn't have much of a choice. If she refused, she would either be shot or pummeled. She knew that very well. She refused to allow that to happen. She wasn't a physically powerful woman, but she had the spirit of a survivor.

Chase flipped the coin—*heads.* He gazed into Harper's eyes and said, "Truth... Do you want to abort your baby?"

The question struck her like a wrecking ball. It was inappropriate, jarring, and disturbing. *How could he ask me something like that? Who does this man think he is?*–she thought. She looked at each and every person in the room—and they all looked back at her. Her eyes stopped on her husband. She couldn't help but cry as she examined his injuries.

Chase said, "Time is running out, ma'am. Do you have an answer for me?"

Harper closed her eyes and, with her voice shaking, she said, "Yes. Yes, I want to abort the baby."

"That's what I thought. Thank you for your cooperation," Chase said, a devilish grin stretching from ear-to-ear.

Brian spat another dislodged tooth at the floor, along with a blob of blood and saliva. He thought about Harper's answer, trying his best to justify it. *She lied to him,* he thought, *she just told him what he wanted to hear.* At heart, however, he knew it was true. He covered his face with his arm and bawled. Harper didn't love him anymore, but she was still human. She felt his pain, so she cried with him.

As he walked back to the entertainment center, Chase said, "I think that was a successful game. Some of you were a little difficult, but we accomplished something with that. It's time to move on, though. We have to check on our last loser."

Chapter Eleven

Numb

Chase took Hazel's revolver. He stood in front of the television and aimed both of the handguns at the guests. Rory tucked his pistol into the front of his waistband as he approached the recliner. He placed his hands on Jackson's kneecaps to stop him from kicking. Backpack slung over her shoulder, Hazel approached Jackson slowly, moving with wide, frolicsome steps.

The crew acted as if they had been there before, nonchalant but prepared. They knew exactly what they were doing and when they were going to do it.

Hazel gently slapped Jackson's cheek and said, "Hey, big boy. How are you feeling?"

"Fuck you," Jackson hissed.

"I wish you would."

Vanessa leaned forward in her seat and cried, "Get away from him." Knowing Vanessa wouldn't stand a chance against any of them, Harper held her back. Vanessa said, "Don't hurt us anymore. Please stop this. We just wanted to have a party. We didn't do anything to any of you. We tried to help you!"

Hazel ignored Vanessa. As a matter of fact, she didn't hear a single word. She knelt down in front of the recliner. One-by-one, she pulled Jackson's feet out of the buckets. Chunks of ice and cold water spilled out during the process, soaking her legs and skirt, but it didn't bother her. She pushed the buckets aside, then she placed Jackson's left foot on her lap.

Eyes glowing with wonder, she said, "Look at this."

Jackson's feet, ankles, and shins turned bright red. His skin suffered from severe ice burns. Some of his toes looked yellow and purple, too.

Jackson's eyes filled with tears unexpectedly as he stared down at his toes. He couldn't feel his feet. He felt a slight tingling sensation inside of his feet, as if ants were scurrying through his veins, but he couldn't feel anything else. He tried to wiggle his toes and twist his ankles, but his efforts were fruitless. His foot just sat on Hazel's lap—*dead.*

Hazel pulled a chef's knife out of the backpack. She stabbed into the bottom of his foot, then she slowly dragged the blade across his rubbery flesh— from his sole to his heel. Blood dripped from the large horizontal gash, but it wasn't as much as expected. The ice restricted his blood flow, slowing his circulation.

As she watched the act in utter awe, Vanessa whispered, "Oh, God..."

Hazel snickered as she examined the cut. She saw white, red, and brown inside of the gash. *Bones? Ligaments?*–she wasn't sure, but she liked the colors. She allowed his left foot to hit the floor, then she repeated the process on his right foot.

As she cut him, she said, "Ice usually helps with certain injuries. It reduces pain and inflammation. It can make you numb to the world. You're not supposed to ice an injury for more than fifteen minutes, though. If you do, it'll cause ice burns or even frostbite. It's worse on your hands and feet because they're, you know, susceptible to frostbite."

"I can't feel anything," Jackson said, his voice breaking.

"I know, hun, I know."

Looking over the other guests, who watched the operation in fear, Chase said, "It's normal to feel nothing, Jackson. You might feel like you lost your feet, but they're still there... for now." The intruders laughed, delighted by the playful threat. Chase continued, "I'm kidding, I'm kidding. As soon as your feet warm up, the blood will start rushing down and you'll feel *real* pain. That's good, too. Real pain will make you understand that there are *real* consequences in life."

Rosy-cheeked, Jackson stuttered, "You–You're insane." He glanced over at his girlfriend, who sniveled in Harper's arms. He said, "Don't look. Close your eyes, baby."

Vanessa didn't want to abandon her boyfriend by turning her back on him. She didn't want to make it harder on him, either. So, she closed her eyes and buried her face in Harper's chest.

Hazel pulled an ice pick out of the bag. She stabbed the sides of Jackson's feet. Droplets of blood oozed out of each puncture wound. Jackson felt a pinch with each stab, causing him to flinch and squirm on his seat. He tried to kick Hazel's face, but Rory kept his legs pinned down. He figured his kick wouldn't do much anyway considering the circumstances.

Hazel turned her attention to his toes. She placed the tip of the ice pick under his big toe's toenail, then she thrust it forward. The toenail cracked and the ice pick penetrated the sensitive skin underneath it. Blood painted his toenail red. He felt another pinch, but nothing else. She repeated the process across all of his other toes.

The other hostages cringed and whimpered as they watched the torture and listened to the *crack* of each toenail. A splinter under a fingernail was bad enough, they couldn't imagine the pain associated with an ice pick under a toenail. They didn't want to watch the torture—it wasn't fun or exciting to them —but their curiosity got the best of them. Humans were naturally attracted to the macabre.

Hazel returned the ice pick to the bag. She smirked as she looked at his toes. The nail beds of his toes were mutilated—sliced and bloody. His blood streamed over his purple, swollen skin. Severed pieces of his cracked toenails fell to the floor.

She said, "That was fun. We need to get to the main event, though."

Hazel pulled a pair of bolt cutters out of the bag. Jackson's eyes widened as soon as he spotted the tool. He thought: *is she going to break my toes next? Or cut them off? What the hell is she going to do?* Unfortunately, the answer to his question was right around the corner. Rory tightened his grip on his legs, ensuring he wouldn't be able to move away.

Hazel opened the bolt cutters, then she closed them over his Achilles tendon. She turned her arms and, in turn, she twisted his heel cord until it ruptured. His heel cord snapped up *into* his leg while blood squirted from his ankle. The blood sprinkled on her arms and clothing, but she didn't stop twisting her arms.

Wheezing and groaning, Jackson gritted his teeth and shook on the recliner. He felt a stronger pinch, then he felt a burning sensation that started at his mangled ankle and ended in his calf muscle. The numbness was dwindling.

Vanessa couldn't tame her curiosity. She peeked over at the recliner. She watched as Hazel closed the bloody bolt cutters over his other ankle. Before she could look away, Hazel turned her arms again, twisting the bolt cutters until Jackson's heel cord was severed with a moist *crunching* sound. Vanessa shrieked at the top of her lungs.

Harper pulled her closer to her chest and said, "Don't scream. Please don't scream. Don't let them know you're scared. Don't make it worse for Jackson, sweetie."

Vanessa couldn't hear her over her weeping, though. Along with the rest of her friends, she whimpered and mumbled incoherently.

Jackson stuttered, "Mo–More blood is–is coming out. It's... It's starting to hurt. I–I need help."

Hazel said, "Don't worry about it, hun. I'm going to do you a favor."

She placed Jackson's feet in the buckets. A few chunks of ice still floated in the bucket, but most of it had melted into icy water. The water quickly turned red due to Jackson's blood, though. The ice was painted red, too. The cold water eased the pain in Jackson's feet and ankles, but the bloody water terrified him. He thought: *can I bleed out from my ankles? Am I going to die?*

Bag slung over her shoulder, Hazel took her revolver back from Chase and returned to her position. Rory followed her lead, acting as if nothing had happened.

As he looked at the buckets, Chase said, "I guess you won't be going anywhere from now on, Jack. Don't try anything funny 'cause it's just going to lead to more pain. Sit back and enjoy the show. If you survive until morning, you might be able to keep those feet. Probably not, though."

As the intruders laughed, Jackson stared down at his lap and cried. Tied to his chair, his feet and ankles mutilated, he didn't have anything else to do. The rest of the group realized the severity of the situation. It was already severe—they were being held against their will at gunpoint after all—but the torture really hit them. They were in danger and there was no way out.

Chapter Twelve

Yakyuken

Still clutching his pistol, Chase munched on a few sweet potato fries and sipped on some wine. He ate the leftovers without a care in the world.

He muttered, "Should have put this in the oven..." He licked his fingers and returned to his stage. He said, "Look at all of you. Sniffling, crying, whining, bitching... I'll be honest: I'm not really digging the atmosphere around here. This doesn't feel like a party at all. So, why don't we lighten the mood? Let's play another game."

The hostages responded with refusal. Like children, they kicked and screamed. They didn't stand from their seats, though. Vanessa's gunshot wound and Jackson's torture stopped them from trying anything too risky. Still, they had to release their rage and frustration somehow. Screaming seemed to be the safest way.

Smirking, Chase said, "Settle down, guys. I've got an idea." He approached the coffee table and looked at Gina. He asked, "You're Asian, aren't you? What kind are you?"

Gina furrowed her brow and cocked her head back. She thought: *what kind am I? What the hell is that supposed to mean? Am I like a product on a shelf to him?*

She swallowed her pride and responded, "I'm Japanese. Japanese-American."

"Japanese. Perfect. I want to play a game called 'yakyuken.' I know it's popular in Japan. Do you know it?"

"I'm Japanese, but I was raised here. I've only been to Japan a few times in my entire life. I don't know yak... whatever it's called. I've never heard of it."

"Really? That's a shame. You should learn more about your roots, Gina. It's an important part of being human."

"I don't think a party game is a big part of my 'roots.' Sorry."

"My point stands. Japan is a wonderful country and you know very little about it. I'm not saying you're wrong, you were raised here after all, but you should still explore your ancestry. It's fun and informative."

Gina narrowed her eyes as she stared at Chase. She didn't understand his speech. She understood his words—his message—but she couldn't read his intentions. He spoke to her as if they were having a normal conversation. The night was anything but normal, though.

Gina said, "I'll make sure to do that when I get home."

Chase responded, "Great. I like that. You're sounding re-energized and confident... This should be fun." He glanced at the other hostages and said, "Let me explain the game to all of you. Yakyuken is basically rock-paper-scissors, except it has a host, music and dancing, and an audience. The loser of each round has to strip off a piece of clothing, too. For our version, on top of stripping, the loser will also have to lose... a *piece* of his or her body. Exciting, isn't it?"

Harper said, "No way. We can't do that. This is just too much. We need to get Jackson and Vanessa to a hospital."

"I need... to go, too," Brian mumbled.

Chase said, "You already know that's not going to happen. You either play or you die. Life or death, those are your only options."

They didn't argue with him. They whispered amongst themselves, they cried and they sniffled, but they didn't fight back. Jackson was barely conscious, Brian had trouble speaking, Vanessa could barely move because of her shot leg, and the rest of them were too scared to act. The odds were stacked against them.

Chase said, "I guess we're playing. Now, it won't be very fun if you strip down to your birthday suit in a turn or two, so let's get the most clothed people to play."

"How about Gina?" Hazel suggested. "She can get in touch with her roots and she's wearing plenty of clothes."

"You're right. She's perfect. We should get a man to play with her, but who?"

As Chase scanned the room for the best candidate, Gina said, "*You.* I'll play against you."

Chase chuckled and pointed at himself. In an uncertain tone, he said, "Me? You want to play against me? Really?"

"Yeah. You're going to force me to play anyway, right? So, why don't I play with you? Or are you afraid of your own games?"

Chase kept a nervous smile on his face. He was surprised by the unexpected challenge. Truth be told, he even felt some fear. It was exciting, though. Gina tried to keep her face as steady as possible. She was scared, of course, but she stood her ground. She wanted to play against Chase just to hurt his crew, even if it meant she would be injured in the process.

Hazel said, "I'm not sure that's a good idea, Chase."

Without breaking eye contact with Gina, Chase said, "I think it's a great idea. We're here to play so we're going to play. *But,* I just ate. I need some time to digest my food before I start having fun. So, Rory is going to play against you instead."

"I am?" Rory asked.

"Yeah, you are. Get over here. I'll watch them from behind. Come on, we don't have all night."

Rory reluctantly handed his pistol to Chase as they switched places.

Before Gina could stand up, Dominic grabbed her wrist and said, "Don't do this."

Gina kissed him, then she said, "I don't have a choice. Don't worry, I can handle it. I love you."

I love you, too—the words were stuck in Dominic's throat. He wanted to stop the game and rescue his friends, but he knew it wasn't happening. There was at least one handgun aimed at him at all times. He watched as Gina and Rory stood across from each other in front of the coffee table, ready to begin the next game.

***

Gina and Rory locked eyes, like two cowboys in a duel. They raised their clenched fists—their right hands—up to their chests.

Swinging their fists down like hammers, they simultaneously said, "Rock, paper, scissors."

The players finally broke eye contact and looked down at their hands. Gina's hand was still clenched —*rock*—while Rory's index and middle fingers were spread wide apart—*scissors.*

As Gina sighed in relief, Rory said, "Best two out of three." He glanced over at Chase and said, "Best two out of three, okay?"

Chase smirked and said, "I don't think so, Rory. You know the rules: take something off, then cut something off."

"Come on, man. You're not serious about this, are you?"

"I'm dead serious."

"This was a–a... a warm-up round. Let's go again."

Pale-faced, Jackson shivered and stuttered, "It–It's your turn, bastard. Get... Get to it."

Chase said, "He's right, Rory. Stop wasting our time and accept the consequences."

Rory let out a loud, frustrated exhale. He removed his jacket and tossed it at the entertainment center. He pulled a boning knife out of the duffel bag. He knelt down, planted his left palm on the coffee table with his fingers spread wide, then he stabbed down at the table beside his pinky. He glanced over at Chase with an uncertain look that said: *are you sure about this?*

Still smirking, Chase nodded at him.

Rory took a deep breath, then, without dislodging the blade, he pulled the knife to the right. The blade cut into his pinky, directly under the distal interphalangeal joint. The sound of his bone *crunching* emerged over his deep nasal breathing. Blood oozed out of the wound, forming a small puddle under his hand. He gasped as he finally severed the tip of his finger.

The hostages watched the self-mutilation in horror and awe. They shared different variations of the same thought: *these people are actually crazy.*

Blood dripping from the end of his mutilated pinky, Rory struggled to his feet. He wrapped his hand around his sweatshirt, hoping to stop the bleeding.

He said, "I... I need some ice. Can you... Shit, it hurts." He nodded at the severed piece of his finger on the table. He asked, "Can you put that on ice for me?"

"No," Chase responded. "Leave it there until the game is over. Keep playing."

"Fine. Let–Let's just get this... over with."

Rory and Gina prepared themselves for another round, locking eyes and raising their fists up. They simultaneously said, "Rock, paper, *scissors.*"

Rory looked at his hand, as if he didn't know what he picked. His right hand was clenched—*rock.* He looked over at Gina's hand and frowned. She threw out 'paper.'

Rory closed his eyes and muttered, "Damn it, goddammit..."

Chase chuckled, then he said, "Another piece of clothing, another piece of your body. Get to it, Rory. We don't have all night."

Rory removed his sweatshirt, revealing the white t-shirt he wore underneath. He knelt down and slapped his left palm on the table again. Blood still gushed out of his cut pinky, squirting out with each twitch. He didn't want to cut off his entire pinky, so he targeted his ring finger instead. He repeated the process: he stabbed down at the table beside his ring finger, then he brought the blade down over the distal interphalangeal joint.

The hostages cringed and whimpered as they watched the horrific scene. The other captors laughed at Rory's pain, entertained by the violence.

Rory unleashed a bloodcurdling scream as he severed the tip of his finger. The pain was insufferable. He felt a tingling sensation across his trembling hand. A cold sweat drenched his lean body and veins bulged from his red face. He loudly swallowed the lump in his throat as he stood up. He teetered a bit, dazed by the pain, but he stayed on his feet.

He wrapped the bottom of his shirt around his hand, soaking it in blood, and he stuttered, "Rou– Round th–three. Let's do it."

Gina was hesitant. She didn't feel bad for Rory, but she feared she was pushing her luck. The game wasn't over, though, so she couldn't stop. *Rock, paper, scissors*—Rory threw out another 'rock' and Gina spread her index and middle fingers for 'scissors.' Gina's face turned cold as she stared at her hand in disbelief. *Idiot,* she thought, *you fucking idiot.*

Hazel said, "I guess it's your turn, hun. Feel free to use any of our other tools."

"Don't forget to take something off, too," Chase said.

Gina removed her coat. She looked into the duffel bag. She found herself looking into a portable armory of deadly tools—screwdrivers, hammers, scissors, a plank of wood, a hatchet, a baseball bat. There were even more weapons buried deep in the bag. Some of the tools were even stained with dried blood.

From his seat, Dominic said, "Don't cut your fingers, Gina. The fingertips are the most sensitive parts of the body and it's going to cause the worst pain. Cut part of your ear instead. It's–"

"Shut up!" Rory barked. He jabbed his index finger at Dominic and said, "You're not supposed to help her. That's cheating. Shoot this asshole, Chase. Shoot him!"

Chase huffed, then he said, "I'm not going to shoot him over that, but you're right. It's cheating, but I didn't make that clear at the start of the game, so I have to let it slide. No more recommendations, okay?"

Gina pulled a pair of scissors out of the bag and teetered back. She didn't realize she was crying until her tears rolled into her mouth and she tasted the salty flavor of sorrow. She looked at her friends, but they didn't look back at her—except for Dominic. She found some comfort in Dominic's unwavering support. *I can do this,* she thought, *we can beat them.*

She opened the scissors over the top half of her left ear, then she closed them. Her eyes involuntarily squeezed shut and she drew a deep breath as the blades sank into her ear. She opened the scissors, then she closed them again. She had to repeat the process ten times in order to cut through the durable cartilage, then the top half of her ear was severed.

The flap fell to the floor beside her foot, along with some locks of hair she had accidentally cut. Blood streamed across her ear and dripped from her ear lobe. Some blood even entered her ear canal. She could still hear, though. Through her gritted teeth, she hissed and cried. She wiped the tears from her eyes, she took several deep breaths, then she nodded. She was ready to continue.

"Oh no, oh no," Harper muttered, shocked.

Vanessa still whimpered in Harper's arms. Brian didn't pay attention to the game. Jackson was still conscious, but he was fading away. Dominic kept his eyes on his girlfriend, though. He couldn't play the game for her, but he refused to abandon her.

Chase said, "Round four. Let's get it done."

The players didn't object. They were determined to hurt each other through a game of pure luck. *Rock, paper, scissors*—Rory threw out 'paper' and Gina used 'scissors' again.

Rory said, "Shit, um... Hand me the scissors. I'll cut my damn ear off, too."

"No, I don't think so," Chase said. "You can use the scissors, but you can't copy her. That's cowardly and boring."

"Are you kidding me? What the hell, man? Why are you doing this to me? I thought we were on the same side!"

"We are. We have to set an example, though. Besides, you just said they were cheating. You wouldn't take advice from a cheater, would you?"

"Fuck you. You're a douchebag, Chase."

Rory removed his bloody t-shirt, leaving him with a thin tank top. He took the scissors and examined his body, searching for the next piece to remove.

Hazel said, "Try cutting off some of your nose. It's already too big anyway."

"No, not the face. I can't touch my face."

He rolled his tank top up to his collarbone and he kept it up with his chin. His nipples were already hard with fear and excitement. He pinched his right nipple and pulled it away from his body. He opened the scissors over his nipple, then he closed them—*snip*.

The severed nipple and the surrounding areola fell to the floor. Blood streamed from the wound on his chest, rolling down his finely-sculpted abs. He stomped and screamed, veins protruding from his face and neck. His chest turned red because of all of the pain and anger flowing through him.

Chase and Hazel laughed at him. They would have clapped, too, but they had to keep their guns aimed at their hostages.

As he recomposed himself, Chase said, "Okay, one more round. Just one more."

Rory and Gina didn't have any other options. They played one final round of rock-paper-scissors.

As they swung their fists down, they simultaneously shouted, "Rock, paper, scissors!"

Gina's rock was defeated by Rory's paper. Rory's eyes welled with tears of joy as soon as he recognized his victory.

He threw a knife at the coffee table and said, "Cut something off with that, bitch." He collected his bag and clothing, then he took his pistol back from

Chase. He glared at Chase and said, "I'm going to get you back for this."

"Yeah, yeah. You just make sure you wrap something around that hand," Chase said, disregarding the threat. He nodded at Gina and said, "Well, get to it."

Gina removed her sweatshirt. Chase *whooed* and Hazel whistled upon spotting Gina's breasts. She wore a black bra, but her perky breasts were still visible. Gina ignored them, though. She looked at every inch of her body and thought about her next move. She thought: *what do I cut? My other ear? My nipple? A finger? A toe?*

As she held the knife up to her ear, Chase said, "Nope. Cut something else. That's too boring."

"Come on, man. Your friend cut two of his fingers," Dominic said. "Have some mercy. She's done enough."

"No. She lost so she has to pay the price."

Gina seriously considered severing one of her nipples, but the idea made her flinch and shudder. For some reason, it reminded her of genital mutilation. She placed her left palm on the coffee table. She cried as she sawed into her pinky. Her friends looked away, unable to watch. The sound of skin *tearing* and bones *crunching* was unnerving. She sawed until the knife scraped the table. The tip of her finger sat in a puddle of blood.

Before she could lift her hand from the table, Chase pulled a butcher's knife out from the back of his waistband, he lunged forward, and he swung the knife down at Gina's left hand. The blade cut through half of her hand horizontally, splitting it in half down the middle. Gina immediately lost control of her pinky, ring, and middle fingers. She fell back, lifted her mutilated hand up to her face, and shrieked.

Dominic yelled, "You bastard!"

He jumped forward and grabbed Chase. He grabbed a fistful of his hair from behind and he yanked his head back, then he struck his ribs with a flurry of hooks.

Hazel aimed the revolver at Dominic and yelled, "Stop it! Get off of him!" She aimed the gun at Harper and stopped her from joining the revolt. She yelled, "Sit your ass down!"

Harper raised her hands over her head and sobbed. Vanessa held onto Harper's arm as she watched the commotion. Brian wrapped his arms around his head and cried.

Then, a gun went off. After a few gasps, an eerie silence befell the room. They looked at Chase's gun, then at Hazels, and then at Rory's.

Rory shot his handgun. His bullet penetrated the side of Dominic's torso, entering his body under his rib cage. The bullet was lodged in his intestines. Dominic grimaced in pain and held his hands over the gunshot wound. He felt a burning sensation in his abdomen and he felt a shocking twinge across his back. He fell back into his seat, overwhelmed by the pain.

The pain in Gina's hand vanished in an instant. She only cared about Dominic. *No, no, no,* she thought, *this can't be happening.* She rushed to Dominic's side.

Gina caressed his cheek and said, "You're okay,

baby. You're fine. We... We're going to go home soon. The night's almost over. We can... We can take a break from everything." She looked down at his bloody shirt. She looked around the living room and cried, "He's bleeding a lot. He needs help. Please help him."

As he walked back to the front of the room, Chase said, "Okay. Hazel, patch him up. I don't want him to bleed out." He looked at Rory and said, "Keep your finger on the trigger, but lower your gun, man. We're not 'trying' to kill these people, remember? We're just here to have fun and this night won't be as fun if we lose everyone before the grand finale. So, take it easy."

Hazel stared at Dominic, trying her best not to smile. His panicked breathing was funny to her. She lifted his shirt, she placed a thin hand towel over the gunshot wound, then she tightly duct-taped the towel to his body. The towel and the tape wouldn't relieve his pain, but the makeshift bandage slowed the bleeding.

The young woman gently slapped his stomach and said, "That should help. Try to stay awake, though. You might die if you fall asleep... or something like that. I think I heard that in a movie once."

Gina slapped Hazel's arms and sternly said, "Get away from him."

"Yeah, sure. Don't you want me to wrap your hand with something, though? You're–"

"Just get away from us!"

Hazel smirked as she stepped away from the couple. She strolled behind the sofa and aimed her revolver at them. She kept them alive only to threaten their lives directly afterward.

Chase felt the tension in the room. Except for Harper, the players were battered, sliced, and shot. He figured they were rightfully angry.

He said, "It's been an exciting night so far. Let's take a breather, okay? I think it's time for an intermission."

Chapter Thirteen

Intermission

Chase dragged a chair from the dining room to his stage. The chair screeched along the floorboards every step of the way, the noise echoing through the cabin. He sat on the chair with the backrest against his chest, like a cliché teacher in a movie. He still aimed the pistol at his hostages, a smile plastered on his face.

He asked, "How are you liking the games so far? Hmm? Are we having a good night or what?"

Dominic and Gina huddled close together, whispering words of comfort at each other. Vanessa was dizzy and lethargic. She had lost a dangerous amount of blood from the gunshot wound on her leg, soaking the cushion underneath her. Harper tried to keep Vanessa awake. Scared but unscathed, she felt guilty because she was the only guest who wasn't injured.

Brian didn't want to play another game, so he kept quiet. Jackson's head was slumped forward, his chin on his chest. He appeared to be breathing, but he wasn't fully conscious.

Chase said, "Well, I think it's been a great night. I'll be honest: this has been the best party I've been to in years—*years.* It's getting late, but we still have a few hours before the clock strikes five. Don't worry, though. I still have plenty of ideas for a few more party games. We could play all weekend if you wanted to. What do you think? Are you up for it?"

Harper cried, "They need help, Chase. Can't you see that? We're shot, we're cut, we're... we're dying. Please leave. We'll call an ambulance and we'll lie to the police about you. You can still get away. Have some mercy."

"You'll lie? For us? *Really?* That's very kind of you, Harper. What are you going to tell 'em?"

"I–I don't know. We'll tell them... We'll tell them someone broke in and robbed us."

"Robbers don't torture people. They won't believe you. If you *really* want us to get away, you should tell them a pack of immigrants—Mexican, African, Syrian, you pick the flavor of the night—broke into your cabin and attacked you because of your wealth. That'll buy us a few days to get down to Mexico. Can you do that for us, Harper?"

Harper furrowed her brow and tilted her head. She thought: *does he really want me to say that? Or is that a trick question?* She didn't know how to respond.

Dominic groaned, then he weakly said, "I think... I'm dying. I can't... I can't breathe."

Chase responded, "As the cops always say: if you can speak, you can breathe."

"It hurts..."

"Of course it hurts. There's a bullet in your guts, man."

Gina placed some gentle pressure on his homemade bandage. She said, "Try not to panic. You know it will only make things worse. I'm okay, you're okay. Everything's okay."

Chase sneered in disgust as he ran his eyes over

his players—*his hostages.* He knew they were injured, but he believed they were exaggerating. He had seen much worse in his short lifetime. *Some of you aren't even hurt that bad,* he thought, *you're all pathetic.*

He said, "Brian and Harper aren't even that hurt, guys. Did any of you notice that? Huh?" He glared at Brian and said, "I guess you two are just better than the rest of these people at everything, aren't you? You just can't stop rubbing it in, can you?"

Brian responded, "I *am* hurt and we're not rubbing it in. You brought it up anyway."

"You're right, but that doesn't make me wrong. You're not nearly as hurt as your friends. You're above them, just like always."

Brian grimaced and asked, "Why are you doing this to us?"

"Why are we doing this to you?"

Chase stared at Brian, eyes burning with disbelief and anger. He quickly stood from his seat, nearly knocking the chair over.

As he paced back and forth in front of the coffee table, he said, "I've told you a million times: we're doing this for fun. But, *no,* Brian needs a better answer. He needs a reason for the madness. Let me explain something to you, moron: there is no reason. What? Huh? You think this is some sort of... art house movie with a deep meaning underneath? You think this is a–a... a Haneke film? You think we're in *Funny Games* right now? Hmm?"

Chase stopped pacing. Red with rage, he scowled at Brian and waited for his response. Brian couldn't say a word, though. The speech caught him off guard.

As he continued pacing, Chase said, "If you actually believe there's a reason for all of this, then you're one naive son of a bitch. You're looking too deep, man—way too deep." He chuckled, then he said, "You're probably one of those dumb shits who thinks Manson was an intellectual, a genius, a–a misunderstood mastermind! Well, he wasn't. He was just another psychopath, just like us. We do our own dirty work, though, and we get *real* dirty."

He paused to catch his breath, to soak in his audience's reaction. He saw the shock and awe on their faces. It stroked his ego, it excited him. He refused to step off his stage until his message was delivered—loud and clear.

He pointed at the television and said, "The news... The media reports on more violence than what's shown in movies. They'll put a mosaic over the gore like the Japanese put mosaics on dicks and pussies, but, just like in Japanese porn, you know it's there—and you can still masturbate to it. I just read about a kid who was murdered by a gang. He was stabbed over a *hundred* times, he was *decapitated*, and his heart was *removed* before he was buried. Why did they do it, Brian? Why would someone do that to a kid?"

Brian said, "I don't know."

"Guess."

"Be–Because he owed money. Maybe he... he stole from them. It was... I don't know, it was probably gang-related."

Chase explained, "There was no reason for it. There is nothing a kid could do to justify one-hundred stab wounds, decapitation, and more. If there was a reason, it would be insignificant. What? The kid stole money? He took some drugs that didn't belong to him? He walked on the wrong turf? He said the wrong words and waved the wrong flag? Those 'reasons' are bullshit."

Hazel said, "We don't need a reason to hurt any of you. We just want to have fun. That's it. At the end of the day, none of it really matters. Life is meaningless, you know? We're all going to die and, once everything turns black, nothing will really matter. The dead won't remember the living and the living won't remember the dead. The only people who will remember the dead a hundred years from now are people who will get caught in Wikipedia 'rabbit holes.' Even then, they won't remember the little people. They'll only remember us: *the killers.*"

"Goddammit," Dominic muttered. He coughed out a haze of blood, then he said, "You're doing this because you're cynical? Because you're having a damn existential crisis?"

"Aren't we all? You're having an existential crisis right now, aren't you, Dominic?" Chase responded. He looked over at Brian and asked, "Aren't you going through the same, Brian?"

They didn't respond. *No*—it was their only answer, but it was pointless. They couldn't argue with their captors, especially with death looming over them.

Rory said, "Fuck this shit, man. Let's just get back to these games. I need to get my head off this pain. My hand hurts, Chase."

Chase said, "Alright, alright. Here's what we're

going to do. Hazel, you keep your eyes on them. If they move, shoot 'em. Rory, get this coffee table out of the way. We need space for our next game." He grabbed the backpack and beckoned to Brian. He said, "Come on, Brian. Let's go to the kitchen. We have to get you ready."

Brian glanced over at Harper, his eyes watering and his lips shaking. Harper looked at him for a second, then she turned her attention to Vanessa. At that moment, he realized he had nothing in the world—just money and the things he bought with it. He felt as if he were marching to the gates of hell as he followed Chase to the kitchen.

Chapter Fourteen

The Piñata

Chase tossed the backpack onto the kitchen island, then he spun in place and faced Brian. He had a conniving smile on his face. The type of smile that said: *this is going to be fun.*

He said, "Brian, I'm going to turn you into a human piñata. If you try anything stupid while we're setting up, I'm going to hurt you, then I'm going to slaughter Harper and your unborn child, and then I'm going to kill you. You deserve it anyway, don't you?"

Brian stared at Chase's chest, purposely avoiding eye contact. He heard the threat, he understood the message, but he was just too tired to respond. He was mentally and physically defeated. The stressful, violent night took a toll on him. And he was broken by his wife's refusal to acknowledge him. *There's no point,* he thought, *I want to die.*

Chase said, "I guess we understand each other."

He opened the backpack and pulled a bag of hard candy out of it—the Jolly Rancher kind. It was a big five-pound bag, but it was already open and some of the candy was missing. Some blood stained the plastic, too.

Eyes glazed with tears, Brian cracked a nervous smile and asked, "Why do you have candy?"

"I'm always ready for a party, Brian."

"What's, um... What's with the blood?"

"We had a little 'accident' during our last party. You've seen the way we play. Some people lose fingers, others lose toes, and a few lose *everything.* Don't worry about the blood, though. You just focus on our game. Get into character, man. You're supposed to be a piñata for crying out loud."

Chase tugged on Brian's button-up shirt, ensuring it was tucked into his waistband. He unfastened the top three buttons, he spread his shirt wide, then he dumped a handful of candy into his shirt. Before Brian could say a word, he spun him around and stuffed another handful of candy down the back of his shirt.

As Chase shoved more candy into his shirt, Brian said, "I don't think you're a good person. You don't sound like a reasonable man. You're crazy. That's the truth. But... I want to make a deal."

"A deal? What kind of deal?"

"You can take my money, my cars, and the rest of my possessions... and you can even take my life. You can do whatever you want to me. No one will stop you from having your demented fun. In exchange, you let my wife and my friends go. Let them save themselves before the irreversible happens. Okay?"

Chase turned him around again, forcing Brian to face him. He pulled a roll of duct tape out of the backpack, then he taped the center of his shirt. He wanted to stop the candy from falling out through the gaps between the buttons.

As he placed more tape on him, he said, "That's very brave of you, Brian, but it's also very stupid. By trying to 'sacrifice' yourself, you'd only be reinforcing their beliefs about you. They already think you're an arrogant, holier-than-thou asshole. Imagine what they'd think if you tried to play the hero that no one asked for."

"I don't care about any of that. I just want to take care of Harper. Even if she left me right after tonight, I would still–"

Chase shoved a handful of candy into Brian's mouth. He said, "Keep your mouth closed. If you open it, I'll open Harper and pull your kid out of her in front of you."

Brian clenched his jaw and nodded. His teeth and gums hurt due to the clobbering he endured earlier with the hammer, but he followed Chase's orders. He felt abandoned by Harper, but he couldn't abandon her. He believed he would die before sunrise. If that were the case, he wanted to fix his relationship with his wife and friends before the end of the night. He sought redemption.

Chase placed a strip of tape over his mouth and said, "Try not to choke on that candy. I mean, do you know how many kids choke on those? *A lot.* It's a fucking health hazard, man."

He spun Brian around again, forcing him to face away from him. He pulled both of Brian's arms back and taped his wrists together several times over, as if he were handcuffing him.

He pushed him forward and said, "It's time to play. Good luck."

***

Chase shouted, "Make way, make way! Here comes Brian, the magnificent human piñata!"

He pushed Brian towards the center of the room —between the recliner and the sofas. The coffee table, stained with blood and littered with severed fingertips, was pushed up against the entertainment center. Rory stood in one corner of the room and Hazel stood in another. Both of them aimed their guns at the hostages.

As soon as she spotted Brian, Harper asked, "What the hell is this? What are you doing to him?"

Chase ignored her questions. He pulled an aluminum baseball bat out of the bag. He placed the bat on the coffee table. He grabbed a fire iron from beside the fireplace, then he placed it next to the bat.

He patted Brian's shoulder and said, "I've filled Brian with candy. It's your job to break it out of him, just like a piñata. You can use the baseball bat or the fire iron, but you can't use your hands. You can't use any other weapons, either. I mean, we wouldn't want you to try to overpower us, would we?" He chuckled and shrugged. He said, "You'll have two minutes to get the candy out of him. Two of you can beat him.... Sorry, two of you can *play* at the same time. Some of you don't look like you'll be able to stand or get a good hit in, but at least you can offer some moral support."

"What happens if we fail?" Harper asked.

"If you fail, you'll be treated like piñatas by Rory and Hazel for thirty seconds each. It may not sound like a lot of time, but trust me, a lot can happen in thirty seconds. Get it out of him. It's better for one of you to take the punishment instead of all of you, right?"

Chase patted Brian's shoulder again. It was the type of pat that condescendingly said: *good luck, buddy.* He walked to the back of the room, ready to watch the show.

He said, "Your time starts now."

Harper looked around, searching for a sense of direction—*for a leader.* She couldn't rely on Jackson's strength due to his lethargic condition. She glanced over at Dominic and Gina. *Dominic is hurt,* she thought, *he won't be able to get the candy out of him, so it's up to me.* She realized it was all part of Chase's devious plan.

Vanessa gently shoved Harper's shoulder and said, "Get him.... Save us."

"I–I can't... I'm not–"

"Fifteen seconds," Chase said. "You've already wasted fifteen seconds. Sixteen, seventeen..."

Harper cried as she finally locked eyes with her husband. Although his eyes were flooded with tears, Brian nodded at her.

Through the tape, he mumbled, "Do... it. Hurry."

Harper ran to the coffee table. She grabbed the baseball bat. It seemed like the most useful weapon against a piñata. Tears dripping from her eyes, she held the bat over her shoulder and screamed, unleashing a ferocious battle cry. She swung the bat with all of her might. She hit Brian's lower back. The *thud* of the bat pounding his flesh was accompanied by the sound of the *crinkling* candy wrappers.

Brian tightly closed his eyes and staggered. He expected a brutal beating, but the blow still caught him off guard.

Harper swung the bat at him again and again— *and again.* One of the swings hit his right arm, cracking his elbow. Another swing struck his abdomen and knocked the air out of him. As he fell to his knees, pieces of candy fell through the gaps between the buttons at the front of his shirt. Harper swung at his back again, but to no avail. She couldn't get the candy out.

Chase said, "You have seventy seconds left. Don't the rest of you want to have any fun? Huh? After everything he's done, after the way he's acted around you for so long, none of you want to hurt this man? Really? That's disappointing. Oh well. The clock is ticking. I hope all of you are ready to suffer the consequences of failure..."

Gina cried as she lurched towards the coffee table. She wasn't motivated by Chase's speech. She didn't *want* to beat Brian, but she refused to allow her captors to hurt Dominic again. She grabbed the fire iron in her only good hand.

She cried, "I'm sorry, Brian! I'm sorry!"

Gina swung the fire iron at his waist. The blow hurt him, but it wasn't enough to release more candy. She cocked the fire iron back, then she swung it down at him again. The hook ripped through his shirt and penetrated his torso between his lowest ribs. She tried to pull the hook out, but it was jammed inside of him. She only expanded the wound with each tug of the fire iron.

Brian leaned forward and breathed deeply through his nose. Each breath sent a surge of debilitating pain through his body. He couldn't tell if all of his ribs were broken or if one of his lungs was punctured. He nearly collapsed, but he knew that would only complicate the situation. He stayed on his knees and endured the beating.

Harper continued screaming as she swung the

bat at Brian's back. She even pummeled his rib cage. The sound of his bones *crunching* and *cracking* echoed through the house.

Gina finally pulled the fire iron out of him, tearing his shirt in the process. The candy came pouring out like quarters from an old coin slot machine. Blood leaked out from the hole, too, raining down on the candy. The side of his shirt was soaked in blood. She could barely see Brian through the tears blurring her vision. She watched as he fell to the floor and rolled to his side.

Weak, Dominic said, "Gina, it's... it's done. Don't... Don't hit him again."

Gina sniffled as she glanced over at Chase. She said, "It's over. We win."

Chase shook his head and said, "Nope. There's more."

"It's over, damn it. We win!"

Chase tapped his lips, then he said, "*There's more.*"

The pieces were easy to connect: the rest of the candy was in Brian's mouth. Gina bent over and reached for his face.

Before she could touch the tape, Chase said, "No hands. You touch him, you get beat."

"How do you expect us to get the candy out of his mouth? Wha–What are we supposed to do?"

"Fifteen. Fourteen. Thirteen."

"Don't just count, you bastard! What are we supposed to do?!"

While Gina yelled at Chase, Harper gazed into her husband's eyes and he gazed back into hers. Brian spoke with his eyes, begging for mercy—begging for forgiveness. Harper was a certain type of survivalist, though: she would do *anything* to survive. She wrestled with her conscience, but she truly felt like she was out of options.

With a shaky, raspy voice, she whispered, "I'm sorry, Brian. I loved you. I really loved you."

With that, the soft glimmer of hope in Brian's eyes was extinguished. He knew it was over. He closed his eyes and nodded, accepting his fate.

Harper raised the bat over her head, then she swung down at him. The bat hit his cheek, creating a vertical gash that stretched from his cheekbone to his jaw. Blood dripped from the tip of the bat as she raised it over her head again. She screamed—a blurt of noise—as she repeatedly swung down at him. A hollow *ping* and a loud *thud* echoed through the cabin with each hit.

Dominic, Gina, and Vanessa watched in horror. Chase, Rory, and Hazel were surprised. No one said a word. The time didn't matter anymore.

After the fifteenth hit, Harper threw the baseball bat aside and bellowed. She placed her palm on her forehead and stared down at her husband. *What have I done?*–she thought.

The left side of Brian's skull collapsed during the beating. Surrounded by cuts, small and large, there was a crater on his temple. His left eye was pushed *out* of his skull, dangling over the bridge of his nose. His entire head was covered in blood. The blood loosened the tape over his mouth. It rolled off his lips, allowing a slimy blob of candy, blood, and saliva to fall out.

Harper held her trembling hands over her mouth

and sobbed. The same question echoed through her head: *what have I done?* Dominic wanted to say something—*anything*—but he could only groan. Gina dropped the fire iron and sat down beside her boyfriend. She leaned on his shoulder and cried. Vanessa thought about life and death, lost in her mind.

Their old friend was dead, murdered in front of them by his own wife. They didn't say a word about it. They *couldn't* say a word about it.

Chase said, "You win. I wasn't expecting that ending, but... *you win.* No plot twists this time." As he walked around the sofa, he said, "I'm sorry about Brian's death. It wasn't on the schedule, but it happened. I think we should just accept it and move on with the night. I think it would be nice if we left him in here with us, though. You know, he can be like a decoration, a reminder, a–"

"No," Harper interrupted. With fresh tears on her cheeks, she glared at Chase and said, "Have some respect, you little brat. Move him. Get him out of here."

"Brat? Did you hear that? She called me a 'brat.' *Me*," Chase said. He stood in front of Harper and said, "I'm not a brat, Harper. A brat is arrogant, ignorant, and annoying. A brat is someone who can't accept the consequences of their actions—like you. You see, you're angry right now and you're looking for someone to blame. You can only really blame yourself, though. You killed Brian for a reason. Because you hated him, because you wanted to control his fate for once, because you wanted another chance at a life of your own."

"N–No. No, I... I did it to win so I could save myself and my friends from you."

"We both know that's a lie. That's going to be your excuse when the cops ask questions, though, isn't it? You're going to tell them the 'bad' people made you do it and you're hoping your friends will support you. Then, when they let you off the hook, you plan on starting a new life with Brian's money. Let's face it: this was your perfect opportunity to hurt Brian. You could have just ripped the tape on his mouth with the fire iron, but you decided to beat him to death. From what I saw, you've been wanting to do that for a very long–"

"Shut up!" Harper shouted as she closed her eyes and tugged on her hair. "Get him out! Make him go away! I won't play if he doesn't go away!"

She wept, snorting and moaning. Her legs wobbled as she walked away from Chase. She didn't look down at Brian, either. She sat down on the sofa, shaking and sniveling. To her dismay, Vanessa leaned away from her. *I saved all of us, but she hates me,* Harper thought, *she's scared of me, they're all scared of me.*

She felt abandoned by her friends, but she understood their fear. Regardless of her intentions, she was a violent murderer in their eyes.

Chase said, "Okay, whatever. This is taking too much time anyway. Rory, move the body to the kitchen. I want to start the next game already."

Chapter Fifteen

Would You Rather?

Life worked in mysterious ways. The night began with an awkward but pleasant reunion party. Then, an innocent act of kindness opened the door to manipulation, intimidation, and violence. Within hours, someone was brutally murdered. In what felt like the blink of an eye, a life was taken away. The frailty of life was terrifying.

The hostages sat in a contemplative silence. They hissed, groaned, and panted, but they didn't speak. They did not communicate in any way.

Hazel said, "I know you've lost a friend and all, but we can't stop playing. It's half past three, so we only have about an hour and a half to play before we leave. And I really—*really*—want to play 'Would You Rather.' It's one of my favorites. Is that okay? Can we play now?"

The hostages didn't respond. They didn't even glance over at Hazel. *Yes, no, maybe*—they knew their answers wouldn't matter anyway.

Chase said, "You're right, Hazel. You're absolutely right. The best way to cheer someone up is by playing a game. 'Would You Rather' is perfect. All of you can stay seated while *we* handle all of the dirty work. You don't have to kill each other this time." He chuckled as he paced back and forth between the seats. He said, "Let me explain our version of the game. To start, I'll be completely honest with you: all of you will be hurt. You'll be tortured, but you won't be killed. We won't take it that far. Each of you will be given two equally painful options of torture, but someone *else* is going to choose for you. It's more exciting that way."

"We can't play," Vanessa said weakly, her eyes on Jackson. "Jackson... needs... help. We're too... too weak to play."

"Don't worry about that. I told you: we're going to handle all of the work. You just need to pick one of two options. Simple, isn't it?"

"We'll... die."

Chase snickered, then he asked, "Well, have you tried *not* dying?"

While Vanessa sniveled, Chase ran his eyes over the hostages and considered all of his options. He thought about starting the game with Harper since she was the healthiest, but he wanted her to suffer on a psychological level. He wanted her to remain unscathed for as long as possible so the guilt could torment her. He decided to play the game in order from left to right.

He said, "We'll start with you, Dominic." Without taking his eyes off the writer, Chase said, "Harper, I want you to choose Dominic's torture. You know, since you're such a cold-hearted killer and all that good stuff. So, would you rather... have your eyeball scooped out of its socket or have your tongue snipped off with a pair of scissors?"

"You're sick," Gina cried. "Please don't hurt him anymore. He's already bleed–"

"Shut up. If you say another word, he'll get both," Chase interrupted. He glanced over at Harper and said, "Pick one or else."

Teary-eyed, Harper looked at Chase and then at Dominic. She feared the consequences of defiance. *I have to pick something,* she thought, *but which one would hurt him less?* Dominic tried to mouth something at her. He wanted to give her the answer to her question. His trembling lips distorted his voiceless words, though.

Upon noticing the gesture, Chase slapped him and said, "No cheating. If you cheat, you'll get tortured with both methods, then we'll kill you. That goes for all of you. Now, Harper, you have five seconds to choose. Five, four, three, two..."

"The eye!" Harper shouted. She sniffled and coughed, disgusted by her decision. She said, "Scoop it out, but make it quick. Please make it quick."

"You heard her, Dominic. One of those gorgeous eyes has got to go. Hold him down, Rory."

"Don't do this, don't do this, please don't do this," Gina pleaded rapidly.

Dominic nervously laughed as Rory grabbed his shoulders and pinned him to his seat. Hazel placed the muzzle of her revolver on the back of Gina's head, guaranteeing she wouldn't try anything stupid. Chase walked to the dining table, he wiped the mashed cauliflower off a spoon, then he returned to the living room with the eating utensil.

Chase said, "To tell you the truth, I'm kinda nervous. I've never done this before, but I'll give it a try. I'll do my best, Mr. Writer."

Dominic said, "Just do it already, you little punk. Get it over with."

"With pleasure."

Chase thrust the spoon at Dominic's left eye at a downward angle. The spoon entered his socket under his eyeball. As Dominic screamed, Chase pushed down on the handle, forcing the eyeball up against the roof of his eye socket. He couldn't pull it out, though. He pushed the spoon *into* his skull until he scraped the back of his socket, then he pushed down on the handle again.

Dominic violently convulsed on the sofa. Rory had to put him in a chokehold to stop him from moving. Gina, cheeks wet with tears, repeated the same phrase over and over: *oh my God, oh my God.*

After a loud *crunching* sound, the left side of Dominic's vision faded. His optic nerve snapped with the pressure and the muscles attached to his eye were severed. Blood cascaded down his cheek like rainfall on a windshield. His eye, crushed at the bottom, rolled out of his socket along with gooey strings of blood, which looked like veins.

As the eyeball fell to the floor, Chase stepped back, chuckled, and said, "Holy shit, it actually worked."

"Oh my God," Hazel said, a kittenish smile on her face.

Rory released his grip on Dominic's neck and moved away from the sofa, awed. Gina instinctively crawled away from Dominic and unleashed a bloodcurdling shriek. She didn't want to abandon Dominic, but she was justifiably horrified. Harper and Vanessa looked away from the couple, refusing to witness the violence.

Dominic held his hand over his face and writhed in his seat. The pain was unbearable—unbelievable, *otherworldly.* He had never felt anything like it before. His mind was addled, thoughts jumbled together and cluttered like trash in a landfill. He could only gasp and squirm on his seat as he waited for the pain to subside.

Gina leaned closer to him. She kissed his hand and his cheek, trying to comfort him with her genuine love. It didn't help much. Chase kicked the eyeball towards the entertainment center. He tossed the spoon at the dining table as he approached Gina.

He said, "Your turn. Since Harper already made a choice and Dominic needs a moment to himself, Vanessa will pick for you." He glanced over at Vanessa and asked, "Would you rather lose a hand or a foot. Pick fast, sweetheart. We're running out of time."

Vanessa closed her eyes and whispered, "Okay, okay."

She thought about her options. The loss of a hand would limit Gina's ability to fight back during the current situation. On the other hand, losing a foot would drastically decrease her chances of escaping. *He already cut up her hand,* she thought, *it might not be as bad if he cuts it off, she might not even feel it as much.*

She opened her eyes and, in a croaky tone, she said, "Take a hand. The cut one."

Chase shrugged and said, "Okay. You're the boss."

Rory put her in a rear naked chokehold.

"Wait, wait, wait, wait," Gina croaked out.

Chase pinned her right hand to the armrest. Hazel handed him a serrated steak knife while keeping her revolver aimed at Harper and Vanessa.

As she tried to pull away from them, Gina shouted, "Dom, help!"

Through the unbearable pain, Dominic heard his girlfriend's pleas for help. He kicked Chase's shin, but the blow barely shook the young man's leg. There was nothing he could do to help.

Chase placed the tip of the blade on her wrist and said, "In some countries out there, people get their hands cut off for stealing. It's usually the right hand that goes first. Repeat offenders lose both. Punishment by amputation is still common, believe it or not, and you get to experience it first-hand... First-*hand,* you get it?"

Vanessa shouted, "Not that hand! The left hand, the injured one! Oh, God!"

Gina said, "Please don't do this. I'm begging you. Don't–"

Chase sawed into her wrist. Blood immediately erupted from the wound and streamed across the top of her hand. The blood dripped from her trembling fingertips and plopped on the floor. The sound of shredding flesh was unnerving. It resembled the sound of a piece of silk being torn—*soft.* Then, a crunching sound followed.

Chase had finally reached the frail bones of her wrist. The blade stopped in her flesh a few times, but he didn't stop sawing.

Holding his breath, he muttered, "Damn it, this is harder than I thought."

Gina shrieked during the entire operation. She jerked every which way, but she couldn't escape her attackers. Loud, hoarse gasps escaped her lips. She struggled to breathe amidst the shock.

A column of blood jetted out of her wrist and landed on Chase's face. He looked away, spat the blood out of his mouth, then he continued sawing into her wrist. He saw red, pink, white, and even purple inside of the gruesome wound. Her fingers locked up and her hand vibrated, but she stopped moving. He knew he was close. So, he sawed into her for another minute.

Eyes wide with fear, Gina watched as her severed hand fell to the floor with a *thump,* leaving a stump at the end of her arm.

"*Finally,*" Chase said. He threw the knife at the dining room, then he dug his fingers into his hair. He said, "Damn, that was hard. Get her a towel or a shirt or something."

Gina panted, drawing short, shallow breaths. She raised her mutilated arm to her face and cried. The same thought ran through her mind: *it happened, it happened, it happened.* Dominic leaned close to her head and spoke to her, but she couldn't hear his words. The world around her was muted. She didn't even hear Hazel as the young woman wrapped a towel around her bloody nub.

Suffering from similar pain, Dominic whispered, "Calm down... calm down. You... You're losing a–a lot of blood, hun. We can't panic. We can't... We can't go into shock. Not now. Please calm down."

Chase didn't care about the couple's conversation. He turned towards Vanessa and said, "Your turn. I think Gina is going to be a little vengeful after what you did to her hand, so we'll let Dominic pick your punishment. Okay?"

Vanessa responded, "I didn't ask for that. No, I

didn't... I told you to take the other one, damn it!"

"I must have misheard you," Chase said. He glanced over at Dominic and asked, "Would you rather be stabbed five times with an ice pick or have your clit snipped off?"

"Goddammit, what's wrong with you?!" Dominic barked. "Oh, God, this can't be happening. It–It can't be real. It can't be..."

"It is. Now make the choice, Dominic."

"I can't! I can't... I can't even breathe. I can't see! Gina, she needs help. Just... Just go away already, kid. Call an ambulance and go away."

"Make the choice or your girl loses a foot."

Dominic struggled to think clearly. The pain distorted all of his thoughts. The sound of his girlfriend's panting didn't help, either.

He said, "The ice pick."

Vanessa let out a shuddery sigh of relief. She was terrified of being stabbed. It didn't seem pleasant at all. Having her clitoris 'snipped' off? That was a completely different story. The mere thought of genital mutilation caused her to cringe and shake.

Chase pulled the ice pick out of the bag. He asked, "You ready for this, Vanessa?"

"I–I'm ready. Do it."

Chase placed his left hand on Vanessa's shoulder and thrust the ice pick down at her torso. The ice pick easily cut through her flimsy dress. He stabbed her five times. The first three thrusts punctured her lower abdomen. He even stabbed her directly through her belly button. Then, he stabbed the center of her torso, directly below her ribs. He ended the attack by stabbing her left breast.

With each stab, he thrust as hard as physically possible, driving the ice pick three to four inches into her. Blood squirted from the wounds each time he pulled the ice pick out.

Vanessa stared down at her little black dress. She couldn't see most of the blood, but she felt it—warm, *plentiful.* She held her hands over her stomach and wept.

She cried, "It burns. I think I'm dying."

Dominic waved at her and said, "Nessa, put pressure on it."

"I–I can't. I'm bleeding from... from everywhere. I'm going to die."

"Don't say that. Please stop saying that."

Chase returned the ice pick to the bag. He pulled out a retractable box cutter. He walked back to Harper and stared down at her—as smug as ever. He placed his filthy boot on Harper's stomach, causing her to gasp and twitch. Her panic excited him further.

He said, "Gina, it's Harper's turn. You're going to make the choice. Hey, can you hear me? Are you listening?"

Dominic gently slapped Gina's cheek and said, "Sweetie, it's almost over. Just make the choice and end this already. Okay?"

Gina breathed deeply through her nose. Her eyelids flickered and her bottom lip quivered. She felt her heartbeat slowing down with each passing second. It was a frightening sensation. Her mutilated arm on her chest, she looked at Chase and nodded—*I'm ready.*

Chase said, "Great. Would you rather have your

stomach *stomped* five times or would you rather have your wrist slit?"

Gina was barely conscious, but she recognized Chase's plan. She figured Chase was purposely trying to pit them against each other by giving Harper the least severe punishments. *He wants me to pick the first one,* she thought, *she probably wants the same, too.* If she picked the second option, Harper could die from a loss of blood. If she picked the other option, Harper could lose the baby—a baby Harper didn't want in the first place.

Pausing between each word, Gina said, "Cut... her... wrist."

Chase asked, "Are you sure about that? She could die if we don't end this soon."

"Do... it. For... For Brian. For the baby."

"Okay, boss lady."

Chase grabbed Harper's left arm. He turned it over, forcing her palm to face the ceiling. The sleeves of her house-dress barely covered her upper arms, so he didn't have to move the garment in order to operate.

As Chase placed the tip of the box cutter on the crook of her elbow, Harper leaned closer to his face and said, "Don't do it. I'll do anything. Okay? *Anything.* I–I'll give you money. I'll... I'll fuck you. You can have my body, okay? Just don't hurt me."

"I'm sorry, baby, but I can't break the rules for you."

Chase pushed the blade into her arm, penetrating her skin with ease. He sliced down her forearm, following a vein to her wrist. He punctured her arm at the crook of her elbow again, then he repeated the process. It was as easy as cutting through a block of warm butter—*too easy,* in fact. He left four long, vertical gashes across her forearm.

Harper's arm trembled uncontrollably. The act of lacerating her arm wasn't as bad as she expected. The stinging pain that followed caught her off guard, though. The mere sight of her blood made her woozy, too. She had never seen so much of her own blood before. She wrapped the bottom of her dress around her sliced arm, hoping to stop the bleeding.

Standing behind the recliner, Chase said, "Unfortunately, it doesn't look like Jackson is with us anymore. His death was premature, but... what can we do? He knew the consequences of failure. At least he outlived Brian... I think?" Smiling, he looked around the room and asked, "I mean, did anyone even notice him die?"

Vanessa looked at her boyfriend and sobbed. Memories of their relationship, good and bad, flooded her mind. She remembered why she loved him—he was handsome, he was funny, he was honest. And now he was dead. Jackson sat in the recliner with his head slumped forward. His eyes were closed, his chest was motionless. The color faded away from his lips and cheeks.

Chase said, "Let's just be sure, though. I don't want him to jump out at us at the last minute like they do in the movies."

He ran the blade across Jackson's throat slowly, cutting him from ear-to-ear. Blood oozed out of the cut. He grabbed his forehead and pulled his head as far back as possible, consequently stretching and widening the wound on his neck. A wave of dark blood poured out of the wound on his throat, racing down his neck and chest.

Her voice raspy from all the crying, Vanessa said, "No, God, no. Jackson, baby... Jackson, I love you."

Although injured, the rest of the hostages shed tears of sadness for their murdered friend. The party crashers gave them a minute to mourn.

As soon as that minute elapsed, Chase said, "Okay, let's move on to the last game. Don't worry, it won't hurt much. It might not hurt at all. It's a classic."

Chapter Sixteen

Russian Roulette

Chase approached Hazel and said, "Give me the revolver. You take my pistol. Don't take your eyes off 'em, babe. They're hurt, but they're not out."

"I got it," Hazel responded.

The couple exchanged handguns. Chase returned to the front of the room. He thumbed the cylinder release latch, then he flicked the cylinder out. He unloaded the cartridges until only one remained. He shoved the rest of the cartridges into his pocket for safekeeping. He spun the cylinder and raised the revolver to his head, touching his temple with the muzzle.

He grinned and said, "We're playing 'Russian Roulette.' I'm going to spin the cylinder of this revolver, I'm going to aim it at your heads, then I'm going to pull the trigger. If you live, you win. We leave, you call 911, and we all live happily ever after. If you lose... Well, you know what happens if you lose. *Bang!*" He laughed along with his friends. He asked, "So, who wants to go first? Hmm? Any volunteers?"

Dominic glanced around the living room. Jackson's dead body was still tied down to the chair across from him. A trail of blood on the floorboards led to Brian's body in the kitchen. The others were brutalized—shot, stabbed, mutilated. There was blood everywhere. *Mayhem,* he thought, *it's all fun and games and mayhem to them.* He was tired of cowering in fear.

Blood leaking from his mutilated eye socket, he said, "Why don't you play with us, Chase? It's the end of the night, isn't it? Shouldn't you go out with a bang like the rest of us? Huh? Put your money where your mouth is, kid."

Rory said, "Shut up. We make the rules around here, not you."

"Rules? Let's stop lying to ourselves, guys. There were never any rules. You planned on playing games and hurting us. That's it. You're not criminal masterminds. You're just demented killers with guns."

"Now you get it," Chase said. He lowered the revolver and approached the sofa, slowly and calmly. He said, "You're absolutely right. We didn't have a long, detailed plan ready for you. In fact, if you kicked me out before we got in here, we would have just moved on to the next cabin. Fortunately for us, you were all a bunch of pussies. I'm not a coward, though. I'm not afraid to die. I'll play with you, Dominic. I'll go round for round against all of you."

Through his gritted teeth, Dominic responded, "Then do it, punk."

Hazel shook her head and said, "You can't be serious, Chase. You don't have to listen to this asshole. He's almost dead."

"I know," Chase responded. "So, I'm going to grant him his dying wish."

Chase bent forward and lowered himself to Dominic's eye level. He raised the revolver to his temple, holding the gun with a steady hand. His cheeks reddened, his nose twitched, and his eyes welled with tears. He looked nervous, but then he smiled—a shameless shit-eating grin. He wasn't afraid, he was just excited.

He closed his eyes and screamed, causing Rory and Hazel to look away and flinch. Then, as his shout reached its peak, he pulled the trigger.

Click.

Chase stopped screaming. He opened his eyes and found himself staring at Dominic. Their eyes were dull with disappointment for different reasons. Dominic wanted vengeance while Chase sought the ultimate thrill through death. Unfortunately for Dominic, the revolver didn't go off. For Chase, the rush of the game—*the high*—dwindled quickly.

Chase spun the cylinder and said, "It's your turn, Dominic. I'll count to three, then... then we'll see if you're as lucky as I am." He placed the muzzle of the revolver on Dominic's forehead, right between his eyebrows. He said, "One, two..."

"Wait, please wait," Dominic said, grimacing.

"Three."

Chase squeezed the trigger—*nothing.* He grumbled about the unsatisfactory results of the game while Dominic cried tears of joy.

Rory said, "Hey, man. I think you should stop playing. You're going to get hurt and... and then what? What the hell are we supposed to do if that happens?"

Without looking at him, Chase responded, "You know what to do. Just stick to the plan."

He sidestepped his way to Gina, who barely clung to life beside her boyfriend. He loaded another cartridge into a chamber, then he spun the cylinder.

Dominic asked, "What are you doing? Two bullets?"

"Yep. It's going to be more exciting this way. We had a one-in six chance of dying when we played. Those odds were too good. I mean, just look at us, Dominic. We're alive, man. So, now we have a one-in-three chance of having our brains blown out. Thrilling, huh?"

"N–No, that's not fair."

"It's completely fair. I'm still playing, so we're sharing the same risks. Let's see how far we can take this."

He put the gun to his head. He took a deep breath, he closed his eyes, and he pulled the trigger. *Click*—he heard that loud *click* again.

"Shit," he muttered as he spun the cylinder again. He placed the muzzle of the gun on Gina's forehead and asked, "You ready?"

In a weak whisper, she said, "Do... it."

"One... two... three."

He pulled the trigger and the gun went off. His bullet smashed through her skull and tore through her brain, exiting through the back of her head and entering the cushion behind her. Bits of her squishy brain burst through the exit wound, splattering on the sofa. Some blood even landed on Hazel's skirt and legs.

Dominic was deafened by the unexpected gunfire. He had heard gunfire before—he was shot earlier in the night along with Vanessa after all—but the revolver was so close to his head. His left ear rang and his brain throbbed for a few seconds. As soon as he recomposed himself, he leaned closer to Gina and whimpered. He shook her shoulder, pinched her arm, and slapped her cheek gently, but she didn't awaken.

He shouted, "Gina! Gina, sweetie, wake up! Don't leave me like this! No, don't... don't let it end like this. Please wake up..."

He kissed her lips, cheeks, and nose. He tasted her blood with each kiss, but that didn't stop him. He hoped his kiss would resurrect her, acting as if he were in some sort of fairy tale.

He cried, "We should have never came to this damn cabin. We should have stayed home. We had everything... everything. Why did this have to happen to us?" He glared at Chase and shouted, "Why did you do it?! Why? Why? Why, damn it?!"

Chase said, "Hazel, watch him. I don't want him to try anything stupid."

"I'm talking to you, bastard!" Dominic yelled. "Answer me!"

Chase didn't respond to him. Truth be told, he didn't have an answer for him. He moved on to Vanessa. He loaded two more cartridges, leaving three in the chambers, then he spun the cylinder.

He whispered, "Now it's getting interesting."

He held the gun to his head. His hand was as steady as ever, but his heart rate accelerated. He felt adrenaline pumping through his veins. The game was extraordinarily dangerous—and he loved it.

Rory turned his head away, but he kept his eyes on Chase. He was afraid of witnessing his foolish suicide, but he couldn't look away. Hazel focused on Dominic, keeping the pistol aimed at his back. She loved watching a good game of Russian Roulette, but she couldn't watch Chase play. She actually cared about him.

Chase pulled the trigger. A loud *clicking* sound broke the tense silence in the room.

Chase said, "I must have a guardian angel. Well, let's see if Jackson is watching over you."

"You're a monster," Vanessa said, tears rolling down her cheeks.

Chase said, "One..."

"We don't deserve this. No one deserves this."

"Two..."

"What's wrong with you?! Why won't you let us go?"

"*Three.*"

As soon as she heard the final number, Vanessa swung at Chase's arm. She moved fast—faster than ever before. She was impressed by her own speed. Chase pulled the trigger and shot the wall behind Vanessa. He teetered back and laughed, surprised and entertained by her sudden act of defiance.

Vanessa stumbled past the sofas. *Run!*—she heard a man yell that word, but she didn't know who shouted it. Although impossible, she chose to believe the message came from Jackson, her guardian angel. She dragged her leg behind her as she reached the hall. She could see the finish line—the front door.

Rory and Hazel tormented her by allowing her to see the front door. She was never going to escape. They shot at her, unloading a hail of bullets. Rory fired five times, Hazel shot at her four times. Vanessa's back was riddled with bullets—*seven,* to be precise. The other two struck the wall beside her.

She collapsed in the hall, releasing one short, panicked breath after another.

Hazel said, "You see, folks, that's why you don't try to run away."

Chase took Hazel's handgun and approached Vanessa. He stood over her and stared down at her, examining every twitch and listening to every groan. She was still trying to move.

Chase said, "You're a fighter, Vanessa, but you're not a very good one. Now look at yourself. You're flopping around in a puddle of your own blood—*dying*. Yeah, you're dying, Vanessa. And the fucked up thing is: there's nothing waiting for you. You will die and you will be forgotten. You're not going to heaven or hell or anything like that. You're not going to be reunited with Jackson. It's not happening."

Dominic knew Chase was psychologically torturing Vanessa. He was trying to terrify her—trying to make her doubt everything—before her inevitable death.

Dominic said, "Don't listen to her, Nessa. It's okay. Just close your eyes."

As Vanessa closed her eyes, warm tears dripping from her face, Chase said, "Go ahead and do that, 'Nessa,' but it's not going to change anything. I'm still going to kill you. Death is still going to come for you and it's going to be on my terms, not yours. You can hide, but you won't live. This is the consequence of your failure."

Chase waited for about a minute, allowing Vanessa to sob and beg. He gave her time to think about death: *what was it like? Did it hurt? Was there an after-life?* Then he shot her in the back of the head. He returned the handgun to Hazel, then he walked back to the sofa. He smiled at Dominic, then he smiled at Harper. Everything was back to normal.

He loaded two more cartridges into the revolver, leaving four rounds in the chambers. He purposely left two empty chambers directly beside each other. That way, there was a *slight* possibility that Chase and Harper could survive the next round without a second spin.

He spun the cylinder and placed the muzzle of the revolver on his temple. He closed his eyes and pulled the trigger, refusing to waste any time. Against all odds, he survived the game. He chuckled and shook his head. *I really do have a guardian angel,* he thought.

Rory said, "Holy shit, man, you're a legend."

"You're the luckiest man on the planet, babe," Hazel said.

Dominic muttered, "You lucky bastard... How did you do it?"

Chase looked down at Harper. He saw the fear in her moist eyes. She would give him all the cash in their safe, she would actually fuck him in order to survive. It was all up to fate, though.

Harper sat with her bleeding arm tucked close to her body. She trembled like a wet dog—confused, injured, scared. There were dead bodies all around her. *I don't want to die,* she thought, *please don't let me die.*

Chase leaned closer to her and said, "It's almost over, Harper. You've done great so far, but I'm afraid it's out of your hands this time. Do you have anything to say before the moment of truth? Hmm?

Is there anything you want to get off your chest? Anything you want to say about Brian?"

Tears spilling from her eyes, Harper said, "Yeah. Yeah, I have something to say. I have a lot to say, actually. Um, where do I start?"

"Anywhere."

"Okay, okay. Well, I stopped loving Brian years ago. I still had love for him, but I wasn't in love with him. I just loved his company and I loved the security he brought to my life. I didn't love *him,* though. I know it would have broken his heart, but I wish I told him a long time ago. The–The baby... The baby probably isn't his, either. I've been having an affair. Yeah, I–I've been cheating on him. God, I'm such a horrible person. I know that. I know it..."

Chase smirked and said, "Scandalous deathbed confessions... It could make a great book or a list on some shitty social news website, huh? Well, I'm glad you opened up to me. Now let's finish the game."

As Chase aimed the revolver at her forehead, Harper said, "Wait, wait, wait. Are–Aren't you going to spin it again?"

"No. We're going to test your luck. I think we both know you deserve it anyway."

Harper leaned back in her seat and closed her eyes. She didn't want to see it coming. She counted to three, and each second felt like a minute.

Click.

She opened her eyes and stared down the barrel of the revolver. She looked down at herself, then back at the gun. She even tapped her forehead. *No gunshot,* she thought, *I'm alive.*

Chase said, "Would you look at that? You must

have a guardian angel somewhere, too. Maybe it was Brian or maybe it was one of these dead suckers... or maybe it was just pure luck. Yeah, luck has a funny way of changing things." He tucked the revolver into his waistband and walked to Hazel's side. He said, "Congratulations, fellas. You won the game. Allow me to apologize for the mess. But, I'm sure Brian is leaving you a fortune, Harper. Give them a day and a handful of housekeepers should have this place looking as good as new."

Harper stared at her captors in disbelief. The group murdered four of them while gravely injuring the other two. Yet, they acted like nothing had happened. They put their weapons away and gathered their bags. Rory grabbed the duffel bag, which now included the fire iron from their human piñata activity. Chase carried the backpack, taking the load off Hazel's back.

Dominic yelled, "Kill me! Shoot me, you little punk!"

Chase stood over Vanessa's body. He glanced back at Dominic and said, "Sorry, bud. That's not how the game works."

"Fuck the game! Shoot me! I... I don't want to live. Don't leave me like this. Kill me. *Please.*"

"The game is over, Dominic. Have a great life, champ."

"Wait, damn it! Wait a goddamn minute!"

Chase, Rory, and Hazel exited the cabin through the front door. Their departure was officially confirmed with the sound of the front door slamming behind them.

***

Harper pulled her cell phone out of her bag. Her hand trembled and her tears landed on the screen. She didn't have service, she could clearly see that, but she still tried to call the police. To her dismay, the call didn't connect. She sent a text message to all of her contacts that read: *911 911 911.* The message wasn't delivered to anyone.

She said, "Dominic, there's no signal. I can't call anyone. I can't even send a text message. What do we do?"

"I don't know," Dominic said as he leaned his head against Gina's shoulder.

A kind of hopelessness was painted on his cold, pale face. He couldn't cry anymore. He was out of tears to shed. He survived the party games while losing his reason to live—he was a winning loser.

Harper said, "We have to do something. We have to get help or... or we'll die."

"I can't move, Harper. I've lost too much blood. I'll stay here with... with Gina."

"Okay, I get it. I'm lightheaded, but I think I'm good. I'll, um... I'll run to one of the neighbors. I'll get help."

"Don't go now. No, not now. They could... They could still be in the driveway waiting to ambush you. Give it a few minutes."

"You'll be dead in a few minutes, Dom!"

"Then it doesn't matter, does it? Your closest neighbor is a mile away. I'm dead either way."

Harper sniveled and glanced around the living room, awed by the carnage. She wanted to get help, but it seemed pointless—everyone was dead. *I can't argue with a dead man,* she thought, *and that dead man makes sense anyway.* She pulled the curtain off the window, breaking the curtain rod from the wall with it. She tore the curtain down the middle, then she wrapped one half of the fabric around her lacerated arm in order to stop the bleeding.

Then she ran back to Dominic. Against his will, she lifted his shirt and examined the damage caused by the bullet. The towel was soaked in blood, warm and heavy, and a cold sweat glistened on his torso. She wrapped the other half of the curtain around his body. Although it seemed hopeless, she didn't want him to die in the cabin. She had lost too many friends throughout the night.

As she tightened the curtain around his torso, Harper said, "I'm sorry. I'm sorry for Gina. I'm sorry for Vanessa and Jackson. I'm sorry for... for Brian. I'm sorry for everything." She laughed—a nervous, broken laugh. In tears, she said, "You probably hate me. I don't blame you, either. I'm... I'm a horrible person. A mean, selfish cheater..."

"You're not... You're not a 'horrible' person. You're not bad, you're just human. You made some mistakes, but everyone makes mistakes. None of this is... is your fault. Not even Brian's death."

"Thank you for saying that. Thank you so much."

The pair hugged on the sofa. Harper cried into Dominic's chest while Dominic gently stroked the back of Harper's head. They spent ten minutes mourning the deaths of their loved ones, apologizing to one another, and forgiving each other. They were devastated by the sheer loss of life in the cabin, but they were still alive. They were ready to fight.

Harper said, "I'm going to make a run for it now.

I'll go to the main road and I'll go... I'll go west. I think the Millers are at their cabin this weekend, so they should be able to help. I'll try to wave someone down, too."

Dominic grabbed her arm before she could stand up. He said, "Don't... Don't go with anyone you don't trust. O–Okay? Look for your real neighbors and for... for cops. Don't fall for one of their traps."

"I won't. I'll be careful. You just stay awake, alright? Whatever you do, don't fall asleep. Please, Dominic, stay with me."

"I–I will. Just stay alive. Good luck."

"Good luck to you, too."

Harper gazed into Dominic's heavy-lidded eye, sharing a nonverbal farewell with him. She patted his arm, then she struggled to her feet and made her way through the living room. She staggered down the hall and headed to the front door, bouncing from wall-to-wall. Her eyes glowed with hope as she reached the front door.

She turned the knob hastily, pulled the door open, and took a step forward. She stopped in the doorway, though. The joy was wiped from her face.

Chase stood on the porch, the revolver clenched in his right hand. His signature smirk—charming but devious—was plastered on his face. Rory stood behind him, leaning back on a handrail, and Hazel sat at the top of the porch stairs. The thugs left the cabin, but they never left the property. They played with their hostages.

Harper stuttered, "It–It can't be. You–You said it–"

"Hello, Harper," Chase interrupted. "It took longer for you to come out here than I thought. I was starting to believe you might have killed yourself. That would have been very disappointing."

"Wha–What are you still doing here? What do you–"

Chase squeezed the trigger twice. The bullets penetrated Harper's baby bump—one below her belly button, the other towards the center of her torso. Harper covered the wounds with her hands and leaned on the wall. She looked down at herself and spotted the blood on her palms. She panted and groaned, panicking.

Still smiling, Chase aimed the gun at her head, but he didn't pull the trigger. Harper could see what he was doing: he wanted to hurt her by killing the baby of her true lover.

From the living room, Dominic yelled, "Harper! Harper, what happened?! Har... Harper, talk to me!" He leaned forward and fell off the sofa. He crawled towards the front door and yelled, "It's you, isn't it?! I... I knew you were still here! You punk! You fucking punk!"

Harper stumbled down the hallway, her hands over the gunshot wounds. She felt a strange sensation in her body, as if all of her organs were twisting and turning over each other. *Something's wrong,* she thought, *oh, God, something's wrong.* She stepped over Dominic. She didn't hear his screams, either. She fell to her knees and leaned back on the three-seat sofa.

Chase followed Harper into the living room. Dominic grabbed his legs and stopped him from reaching the sofas.

Dominic looked up at him and said, "Get... out.

Don't... touch her."

Chase responded, "Sweet dreams, Mr. Writer."

He stomped on the back of Dominic's neck, killing him instantly. His spinal cord snapped with a loud *crunching* sound. His airways were crushed upon impact, too. His head was cocked up, planting his chin on the floorboards. Blood dripped out of his mouth. He died right next to Vanessa. The killer kicked Dominic's arms away, then he moved forward.

Chase said, "Let's finish this."

Harper stayed on the floor, her head slumped back on the couch cushion. Her vision blurred and darkened, but she could still see. She watched as Rory entered the bathroom. After a few seconds, he returned to the dining room with a small device in his hands. The black device had three antennas protruding from the top.

Harper thought: *it's a cell phone jammer, that's why we weren't able to call anyone.* She figured Chase or Rory planted it in the bathroom earlier in the night. She heard a door hit a wall, followed by grunting and groaning. She glanced over her shoulder and stared at the kitchen door.

Chase and Hazel carried Brian's body into the living room. They set the body down beside Harper, pushing his bloody, crushed head onto her shoulder.

Harper whimpered and said, "We won. We... We beat you. What are you doing here?"

Chase knelt down in front of her. He said, "We're finishing what we started. Don't get me wrong: *you're right.* You won the game fair and square. The problem is: I don't like losing. So, we decided to kill all of you. That way, we can tell people we won anyway. That's the way it is. The person with the biggest gun makes the rules and writes history, right?"

Hazel patted Harper's head, as if she were petting a dog. She said, "It's okay, baby. You lasted longer than most people. Look at the bright side, too. At least now you get to die with the man you vowed to die with, instead of that person you cheated with. It's kinda honorable, right?"

Chase aimed the revolver at her head and asked, "Any last words?"

Harper said, "I... I just... I want to apologize for–"

Chase pulled the trigger. The bullet entered her head through the bridge of her nose and became lodged in her brain. Her head fell to the side, her cheek leaning against Brian's wavy, bloody hair. Dead bodies filled the living room. The furniture, floor, the ceiling and the walls were painted red with blood. The acrid, metallic scent of blood stained the cabin, too.

Chase stood up and handed the gun to Hazel. As he stared down at Brian and Harper, he said, "Game over. Let's get out of here."

Chapter Seventeen

The End

Chase, Rory, and Hazel departed from the cabin. Chase strapped the backpack onto his shoulders, Rory lugged the duffel bag, and Hazel walked a few feet ahead of them. The clock barely struck five. The forest was still dark, solely illuminated by the stars and moon. A cool breeze caressed their bodies while the mist from the nearby lake surrounded them.

Hazel looked up at the neighboring trees and said, "Sun should be up soon. Maybe in an hour, maybe less."

"It took longer than I expected," Rory said. "Those assholes were stubborn and lucky."

Chase responded, "Yeah. We're good, though. We have plenty of time."

He glanced over his shoulder and peered at the cabin. From the outside looking in, it resembled a normal vacation home.

He said, "There were six of 'em, so of course it was going to take some time to kill 'em all. They were lucky, too. They were very, very lucky. I've never seen someone survive Russian Roulette the way we did. It's just... insane."

Hazel said, "Luck couldn't save them, though. I mean, what good is 'luck' when you still die in the end?"

"You're right, baby. Luck is all about perspective. We were lucky to meet them, but they weren't lucky to meet us."

"Yep. Fuck luck."

The young killers walked down the side of the road. An SUV whizzed past them, but they paid it no mind. After a ten-minute walk, they took a right and strolled into the woods. They didn't follow a path. They walked for less than a minute before they stumbled upon a silver sedan, which was parked between two leafy bushes.

Chase said, "Put the bags in the back with Hazel. I'm driving. Hurry up."

The group followed his orders. Hazel lay in the backseat of the vehicle, using the backpack as a pillow and the duffel bag as a footrest. Rory sat in the passenger seat. He pulled a gauze roll out of the glove department and wrapped it around his mutilated fingers. Chase sat in the driver's seat. He checked his reflection on the mirrors—still as handsome as ever—then he reversed out of the forest.

They cruised down the main road, following the speed limit without jerking or swerving around. They drove past Brian's cabin, unperturbed by their crime. About a mile away, they turned and drove into the forest again. The car jerked left and right as it rolled over the bushes, branches, and holes. It rolled to a stop behind a tree and a bush.

Chase pulled the key out of the ignition. He asked, "Are we all good? Hmm? None of you are hurt, are you?"

Rory huffed, then he said, "Look at my hand, man. I'm... I'm still leaking. I think I need to go to a hospital."

"For what?"

"I cut my fingers off! I'm bleeding!"

"Alright, alright. Calm down. There's no need to yell. I just meant... there's no point, Rory. We didn't bring your fingertips with us and they weren't going to be able to reattach them anyway. They can't make them grow back, either. Look, it's not that bad. Keep some pressure on it and you'll survive. We'll cauterize them later. Okay?"

Hazel hit the back of Rory's seat and said, "Yeah. Stop screaming, too. I'm trying to rest back here."

"Whatever," Rory muttered.

Chase placed his cell phone on the dashboard. He said, "The alarm is set for five in the afternoon. Let's eat and sleep. We're going to need our energy."

The friends munched on trail mix, beef jerky, cheese sticks, and candy bars while discussing the night. They didn't talk about the murder, though. They spoke about the gourmet meal Chase ate when he joined them for dinner. They also spoke about the fancy cabin, discussing the possibility of actually renting one for themselves. They didn't feel any remorse for their gruesome actions.

After their meal, the killers fell asleep in the sedan. The sound of groaning trees, rustling bushes, and passing cars did not disturb them. They dreamed about party games.

***

The sky was painted with dazzling tints of red and blue. Rays of golden sunshine penetrated the trees and dawned on the sedan. The sun slowly fell beyond the horizon, announcing the imminent arrival of nighttime. The cell phone vibrated across the dashboard while emitting the sound of chirping birds. The buzzing sound of the phone's vibrations was as loud as the alarm.

Chase groaned as he awoke. He turned off the alarm and said, "Get up. It's time to work."

Hazel turned over in the backseat and said, "Five more minutes."

"No more minutes, baby. If we want to have fun tonight, we have to get started now."

"Okay, babe, okay. I'm with you."

Chase nudged Rory's arm and said, "It's your turn, Rory."

Rory looked at Chase, eyes wide with disbelief. He raised his mutilated hand and shook it at him, as if to say: *do you see this?* The bandage looked black because of the dried blood.

He said, "I can't go out there like this, man. Look at my hand, look at my clothes. I have blood all over me. I'll probably scare them before I even get inside."

Chase responded, "You can improvise. Tell them you were in a car accident, tell them you cut your hand on glass or you got it caught on a door, tell them anything. You know how to play the game."

"Stop being such a baby," Hazel said as she ruffled Rory's hair.

Rory leaned away from her, irritated. He looked at Chase, then at Hazel, then back at Chase. He was pushed into a corner.

He said, "Okay, I'll do it. *But,* if we play yakyuken again, it's Hazel's turn to take the lead. Deal?"

Chase glanced back at Hazel and asked, "You okay with that, babe?"

"Yeah, yeah, whatever," Hazel said as she leaned

back in her seat. "I'm a pro at rock-paper-scissors anyway. You just have to pay attention to your opponent. It's all in the eyes."

Rory reached into the backseat. He retrieved a pocket knife, a cell phone, and a cell phone jammer from the backpack. He covered all of his bases.

As he climbed out of the car, he muttered, "This is bullshit."

He slammed the door behind him, irked by his friends' laughter. He stumbled out of the woods, his arms crossed and shoulders slumped. A sedan drove past him, then a pickup truck, but no one stopped to help him. *So far, so good,* he thought. He walked down another driveway and approached a two-story cabin. The exterior resembled Brian's cabin, but it didn't have the same affluent flair.

Rory knocked on the front door. He kept his right arm crossed over his chest and leaned on the wall to his left. He tapped his foot and glanced around, waiting impatiently for someone—*anyone*—to answer the door. No one answered, though. He rang the doorbell, he knocked on the door, then he rang the doorbell again. *Open up,* he thought, *come on, we don't have all night.*

As he reached for the doorbell once more, the front door swung open. Janice Miller, an elderly woman, stood in the doorway. The smile was wiped from her round, wrinkly face as soon as she spotted Rory's wounds and bloody clothing. She took two steps back, the tips of her fluffy house slippers gliding across the floorboards. She held her hand over her chest, directly above the flower stitched onto her house-dress.

Rory's eyes drifted up to the short woman's head. For some odd reason, her short, gray hair was amusing to him—maybe it was the perm. He stopped himself from laughing, though.

He said, "Sorry to bother you this evening, ma'am. You see, I was just in a car accident and I'm hurt. I'm not dying or anything, but I could use some help."

Wide-eyed, Janice said, "Well, I can see that, young man. I may be old, but I'm not dumb or blind. Where are you coming from? Where is your car?"

"It's on the main road, about half a mile past your driveway."

"You look... *bad.* Are you sure you should have walked over here like that? You're not dizzy or sick? You didn't hit your head, did you?"

"No, no, no. I've got some cuts, some bumps, and some bruises, but I think I'm okay. I didn't hit anyone else, either. I hit a... a tree."

Janice glanced over her shoulder, then back at Rory. She said, "Okay, well... I'll call 911."

Before she could move away from the door, Rory said, "Wait a second, ma'am. You see, I already called 911. I spoke to... to Officer Brown. He told me they wouldn't be able to get out here for another thirty to forty-five minutes. He said I should seek shelter at the closest cabin in the meantime. Your cabin happens to be the closest to my little accident. Can I rest here? Just until the police and paramedics show up?"

Janice puckered her lips as she thought about the situation. She was disgusted by Rory's injuries and skeptical of his intentions. At the same time, she could not in good conscience turn him away. *What if he's innocent? What if this happened to one of my kids?*–she thought.

Rory looked into the house and Janice glanced over her shoulder. The sound of rapid footsteps and innocent laughter emerged in the cabin. Two blonde-haired kids—a four-year-old girl and a six-year-old boy—ran across the living room in their swimsuits.

I have to set an example, Janice thought as she watched her grandchildren, *I have to teach them to be compassionate.*

Rory wasn't dissuaded by the presence of the children. He was actually delighted to see them. He thought: *tonight is going to be very, very interesting.* Kids loved party games after all.

He asked, "May I use your bathroom? I need a moment to clean myself up and, to be honest, I *really* have to pee."

"Oh, okay," Janice said, smiling and rolling her eyes. She opened the door completely, stepped to the side, and beckoned to Rory. She said, "Come in. I'll show you to the bathroom, then I'll get you some water. My son should be home soon. He'll know what to do about everything else."

"Great. I can't wait to meet him," Rory said with a big grin on his face.

Rory limped into the house, ready to restart the cycle for another night of fun and games.

Join the mailing list!

Want to play some more party games? Are you a fan of dark, provocative, and gruesome horror? Do you want to continue exploring the darkness of the human mind? Well, I have some great news for you. I release dark, disturbing horror books on a monthly basis. During some months, I even release *two* extreme horror novels. I occasionally release supernatural and psychological horror novels, too. By joining my mailing list, you'll be the first to know about new releases and deep discounts. The process is simple and *free!*

By the way, you'll only receive 1-2 emails per month. You *might* receive three emails a month every now and then, but that's not common. You won't get any spam, either. Click here to sign-up: http://eepurl.com/bNl1CP

Dear Reader,

Hey! Thanks for reading *Party Games.* If you're a long-time reader, you're probably familiar with the format of this letter: this is the part where I apologize to any *new* readers who might have been offended by the contents of this book. As usual, there were **warnings** everywhere—the product page, the front matter, and the back of the paperback. If you ignored those warnings or if you missed them, and if you were offended, I'm genuinely sorry. As I've said before, I write to entertain, terrify, and even shock, but I don't write to purposely offend people. I'm not some 'edgy' teenager.

Party Games was inspired by Michael Haneke's *Funny Games,* which I actually referenced in this book. If you haven't watched it, you should. The original 1997 version of the film is excellent. It has some slow moments, but it's very provocative and compelling. I watched it years ago—around my junior year of high school, I think—and I never forgot it. If you're not a fan of reading subtitles, the film also has a frame-by-frame remake, which was also really good. It's not a film for everyone, I know some people who absolutely hate it, but it is worth watching if you've never seen it.

My novel, *Party Games,* is far more violent than *Funny Games,* though. Although the concept is similar, I didn't want to copy-and-paste Haneke's work. I didn't even really want to focus on the same themes, I just really liked the tone and concept of the movie. Beyond it's bloody surface, my book is about random acts of violence, luck and chance, and the desensitization of society. I didn't want this to be a book that preached, though. Like I've always said, I aim to entertain first-and-foremost.

I was also inspired by home invasion movies, which I also referenced in this book. I like the genre. I especially enjoy the French movie *Inside.* I decided to use the skeleton of a home invasion movie while avoiding some of its cliches and pitfalls. I probably failed, but that's what I *tried* to do. Too many home invasion movies rely on characters wearing animal masks and standing in the background for prolonged segments of time. I didn't want to do that.

Anyway, if you enjoyed the book, *please* leave a review on Amazon.com. I am writing this on my knees, begging you to leave a review in advance. Your review will help me improve on my writing, it will help me pick what I'm going to write next, and it will help other readers find this book. Good or bad, your reviews lead to more books that are better than the previous ones. If you need help getting started, here are some questions you can answer in your review. Did you like the story? Did you like the characters? Do you like my short, violent novels? Do you prefer something longer and more complex? Would you like to see a sequel to this book?

If you really want to help, you can show more support by sharing this book. Post a link on

Facebook or Twitter, share the cover on Instagram and Snapchat, write a post about it on your blog, buy a Kindle copy for a friend, or send a paperback to a pen pal. Sharing books is an excellent way to support independent authors and it's also a great way to make friends. By the way, if you buy the paperback of any of my novels, you get a *free* Kindle copy. Isn't that awesome?

Again, if you're a long-time reader, you know what to expect: this is the part where I update you on my financial status for the sake of transparency —and for fun. Well, I'm pretty much in the same position as last month. Off my writing, I make *a little* more than a full-time McDonald's cashier before taxes. And, honestly, I'm extremely grateful for that. I know it's nothing to write home about, especially compared to some of the bigger independent authors out there, but I'm happy. I mean, I'm sad sometimes, but I'm pretty happy with my current position. Thank you for your support. It means the world to me.

Finally, if you're a horror fan, feel free to visit my Amazon's Author page. I've published nearly two dozen horror novels, a few sci-fi/fantasy books, and some anthologies. Want to read a violent story of abuse? Check out *Grandfather's House.* Looking for a twisted tale filled with serial killers, twists and turns, and plenty of extreme violence? Check out next month's release, *The Good, the Bad, and the Sadistic.* If you're new to my books, feel free to check out some of my older novels, too. If you've already read my other books, you know the drill: I release a new book every month, so keep your eyes peeled. Once again, thank you for reading. Your readership keeps me going through the darkest times!

Until our next venture into the dark and disturbing,
Jon Athan

P.S. If you have any questions, you can contact me directly by using my business email: *info@jon-athan.com*. You can also contact me through social media via Twitter @Jonny_Athan or my Facebook page. Thanks again!

Made in the USA
Las Vegas, NV
22 March 2025